ETCHED IN THE MOUNTAINS

Broken paths, wiser hearts

Ryan Fernandes

Dedicated to

My sons, Nihaan & Evaan
May you both always do good to others

Chapter One

"Scalpel, please!" Rhea said.

It was more of a demand than a request. The scrub nurse assisting her hurriedly offered her the scalpel in a kidney tray, which Rhea impatiently grabbed and placed a clean, crisp vertical incision in the centre of the patient's abdomen. She then deepened the incision, and within no time, the intestines popped out of the abdomen like a jack in a box.

Rhea paused and looked at the CT films displayed on the wall in front of her and then got back to localizing the tumor and the lymph nodes in the abdomen. She snatched the cautery from the bag placed by the side of the patient and began devascularising the part of the intestine invaded by the tumor.

"Intestinal clamps!" she commanded when she was done with it.

The scrub nurse assisting her, who had beads of perspiration on her forehead throughout the surgery despite the air-conditioned operation theatre complex, was caught unawares by the abruptness of the command and, in fright, handed her the wrong instrument. Rhea's flared nostrils behind her mask and bloodshot eyes due to lack of sleep made her look downright scary. She grabbed the instrument and flung it across the operation theatre, narrowly missing another nurse standing on the far side.

"Are you incompetent or just too stupid to work

here?" thundered Rhea, bringing her face within inches of that of the nurse, who was on the verge of tears.

"It is because of incompetent women like you that the reputations of all other women get tarnished, and we have to play second fiddle to men forever. I will transfer you to the hospital cleaning department because that is the only place you can work in," she screamed.

That was enough for the nurse to break down even though Rhea would not make good on her threat. Satisfied with the reaction, Rhea pulled out the instrument from the tray herself and completed the surgery amidst the deathly silence of the operation theatre, broken only by the hissing and beeping ventilator.

An hour later, when the surgery was completed, Rhea pulled off her gloves and got out of the scrubs while dictating the post-operative orders to her assistant. She then washed her hands and headed to the changing room, where she sat down on a plush white sofa to relax her aching legs. This was the 3rd case she had operated on since the previous evening, with two emergency cases having arrived back to back. She drank a few sips of the bottled water from the cooler in the changing room, stood up, and looked at herself in the full-length mirror on the wall, unimpressed. She had put on some weight in the last year, though not significant enough to be called *fat*. Back in 12th grade, she was popular for her looks and attracted the attention of many boys in her class. With high cheekbones, a pointed chin, brown eyes, brown shoulder-length hair, and a dusky complexion, she always had her admirers. But over the years, while she studied medicine and more so now after becoming a consultant in the hospital, she could never devote time to fitness, and it was showing. She brushed off the thoughts about her looks and got into her hospital attire: black formal pants, a pink shirt, and a black blazer.

When she left the OT complex, it was just 10 AM, but the hospital was already abuzz with activity, and she loved it. Being part of one of the largest private hospital chains in the country gave her goosebumps. White Arc Hospital's Mumbai branch was a premiere one with every conceivable medical facility available. It comprised six elegant buildings over a 10-acre campus on the city's outskirts. With white marble floors, pale white walls adorned with paintings of flowers & mountains, plush white leather waiting chairs, and false wooden ceilings through which bright LED lights illuminated the hospital, it looked more like a 5-star restaurant with the lingering scent of iodoform being the only reminder of it being a hospital.

As she exited the operating theatre complex, she walked along the passage on the second floor that overlooked the reception area below. She noticed patients and their relatives queuing up behind the ten registration counters, just like at an airport terminal. Each counter had a hospital chaperone dressed in a blue safari suit, who would accompany the patients to their respective outpatient departments and the laboratory for necessary blood investigations and even look after their needs like coffee and snacks. It was an excellent service for those who fell ill, but the cost was exorbitant, a price that many would shudder to imagine. After all, the mammoth campus, hundreds of doctors, nurses, clerical, and other staff would not pay for themselves.

Just as she was about to enter the Department of Surgical Gastroenterology, where her cabin was situated, her phone buzzed. She was surprised to see Dr Subhash Gupta's name flash on it. She swiped her thumb across the screen and put it to her ear.

"Good morning, sir," she said.

"Good morning, Dr. Rhea. I want to speak with you right now," he said.

He didn't bother asking her if she was busy. Rhea hung up and immediately retraced her steps back to the elevator. She tapped her foot impatiently, her black heels clacking against the cold marble floor as she watched the numbers above the elevator door change from 5 to 1. Once she got in, she pressed number six and wondered why in the world he wanted to see her. Dr Subhash Gupta was referred to as the managing director or MD, who looked after the entire White Arc Hospital Mumbai division. He was swamped and called on the doctors only if it was essential. In fact, after her job interview three years ago, he had never spoken to her personally. His secretary conveyed any hospital-related communication to her. *Did he want to congratulate her on the surgery that she had just performed?* But she brushed off the thought, knowing it was too routine a surgery for the hospital's Managing Director to bother about.

After the elevator reached the sixth floor, Rhea quickly walked toward the MD's office. The entire floor was dedicated to various board members' office suites and a large boardroom, which Rhea had yet to see from the inside. She had been curious about its appearance and even tried to open the door once, but it was locked. The ceiling had hidden speakers that played instrumental music softly. The yellow-tinted lights replaced the white ones on the lower floors. The walls were covered with wallpapers and decorated with abstract paintings that made no sense to Rhea. The atmosphere was that of a corporate space and a fruity air freshener instead of the smell of Iodoform.

When she arrived at the door to his office, his

secretary, seated at the desk outside, looked up.

"He is expecting you, ma'am," she said, standing up with a smile.

The secretary then opened the office door and announced Rhea's arrival. Receiving the affirmation from within, she held the door open for Rhea, who entered and then shut the door behind her, leaving her alone with the most powerful man in White Arc Hospital.

As expected, the MD's office was quite spacious. Its theme was based on *brown*, which contrasted with the otherwise white hospital. The room had floor-to-ceiling French windows with a tint, providing a panoramic view of the White Arc campus. Rhea could see the Oncology, Cardiology, and Neurology wings surrounding a massive fountain in the centre. Inside, opposite the window, was a large wooden bookshelf with hundreds of textbooks and journals arranged neatly. In the middle was a large Mahogany table on a soft brown carpet with a single sheet of paper and a pen. Behind the table was a large man dressed in an elegant brown suit and maroon tie. He had a bald pate and wisps of white hair around his temples. Although he was in his late sixties, he still had a physique that did justice to the orthopaedic surgeon he once was. However, he no longer operated and instead looked after the hospital affairs.

"Take a seat," he said in a firm voice, adjusting his gold-rimmed spectacles.

Rhea was one of the toughest women in the hospital, if not the toughest. She was respected for her surgical skills but feared by all for her temper and pragmatic attitude. She was afraid of no one, but something about the MD made her apprehensive, something she was not accustomed to. She sat down in the brown leather chair.

"I'll come straight to the point, Dr Rhea, because I am sure your time is precious," he said.

Rhea knew he meant that the time he could devote to her was limited, and he had more important affairs to attend to.

"As you know, ours is a large and prestigious organization. We pay our doctors handsomely, which you know through the pay cheques you have been receiving for the past three years," he said, placing his elbows on the table.

Rhea was surprised that he remembered that she had worked there for three years. But he was right. They had appointed her as a part of the surgical gastroenterology department right after she had completed her studies with no prior experience to show for, with a massive pay cheque, something surgeons her age could only dream of. Of course, she had an impressive CV, having been a gold medallist in practically every subject during her MBBS, then doing her MS and McH in surgical gastroenterology in two of the premier institutes in the country.

"During your appointment, we informed you that we needed numbers from you. Being a surgeon, that meant the number of surgeries you performed in a day, week, month, and year," he said tersely. "And I am sorry you are way short of our expectations."

Rhea was surprised by his statement. She worked tirelessly, seeing patients in the OPD, attending emergencies, and performing surgeries at any time of the day and night. She had been working so hard that she had no time for herself or her family. She had not taken a single day off in her three-year stint for fear of losing patients to her two senior colleagues in the department. Rhea was mindful that no matter how good she was at her work, patients were always drawn to older, balding men like a moth to a flame.

"But I have given my heart and soul to this hospital, sir," she said, getting unusually emotional.

"That doesn't translate into profits, does it?" asked the MD, unimpressed.

Rhea silently stared at him, not knowing what to do next. His face was indecipherable, and the grey moustache and wrinkles around his eyes betrayed no emotion. *Was he going to fire her?* If he did, she didn't have any dearth of job opportunities in the city because there were enough corporate hospitals that would give an arm and a limb to include her in their setup. Still, she knew they were nowhere close to White Arc in prestige and salary packages. Added to that was the humiliation of being dumped by the premier institute in the country.

"You have excellent credentials, and we believe we can give you more time to achieve our goals. If you can level up, we can continue our association. But if you can't, then I am afraid that we must let you go and appoint someone else since the applications for your post are piling up," he said, picking up a thick bundle of papers from his drawer and placing them on the table of what she assumed to be the resumes of surgeons. She didn't doubt it because there would be no dearth of surgeons vying for her position.

"Thank you, sir," she said, "I will try my best to meet your expectations."

"I am happy to hear that. That will be all," he said, leaning back on the chair.

That was her cue to leave. Rhea stood up, and momentarily, her eyes fell on the vast number of degrees hung on the wall behind him. *How many hours a day had he worked during his time to now sit comfortably in that chair and threaten juniors like her*? How many hours a day would she have to work to do the same to someone else one day?

As she reached the door, she heard the MD's voice behind her and turned around.

"And one more thing, Dr Rhea. Like I said, we see great potential in you, and I hope you achieve the targets we desire," he said calmly and with a smile.

"By fair means or foul," he added with that same indecipherable look.

There was something sinister in his tone that made Rhea uncomfortable. In simple words, he meant to do something *by hook or crook*. She nodded her head and left the room.

Chapter Two

After leaving the MD's office, Rhea chose to walk down the stairs instead of taking the elevator. She wanted to clear her head and gather her thoughts. Rhea was unwilling to let go of her job at White Arc so easily. It was prestigious and lucrative, and she was well-known among her friends and family as a surgeon at the hospital. She had given several health talks on various news channels and medical conferences as a part of White Arc and earned a certain level of respect for herself as a surgeon there.

Rhea had a burning desire to become one of the leading women in surgery in the country, which was otherwise a male-dominated profession, and she believed that White Arc was the perfect place for her to achieve that goal. The money was an added benefit. If she continued to work in the same capacity at the hospital for another ten years, she would become one of the country's most reputed gastrointestinal surgeons and earn enough to retire comfortably in her late forties. However, retirement was the last thing on her mind at present.

She was lost in thought, and before she knew it, she had made her way to the Department of Surgical Gastroenterology on the ground floor, where her cabin was situated. She opened the glass door and entered a massive air-conditioned waiting area bustling with activity. Almost every chair was occupied by patients holding files, CT scan films, and X-rays. Nurses were ushering the patients individually to different cabins, juggling the ever-ringing phones at the counter, and pacifying impatient patients. Patients, both young and old, were all gathered there waiting for their turns, with grim expressions and worried about the judgement that would be passed on them by the doctors inside. Rhea's cabin was on the right-hand side of the waiting area, and on the left were the cabins of two of her senior colleagues. She felt disappointed when she saw more patients seated in front of their cabins than hers.

She strutted into her cabin and instructed the nurse to usher in her patients. She put on the crisp white doctor's apron and sat behind her white desk, and patients began trickling in. Some of them were the ones she had operated on previously and had come for a follow-up. There were a few with vague complaints, which were worsened by a Google search on behalf of the patient and required nothing more than just reassurance. She spent most of the morning frustrated as she did nothing but dole out advice and prescribe medications.

Somewhere close to lunchtime, Rhea's spirits lifted when a middle-aged couple sat in front of her with CT scan films, which Rhea studied carefully and deduced to be a case of cancer of the gall bladder, which would require surgery. She explained in great detail to the patient, a 42-year-old woman in a yellow saree, and the husband about the disease and the surgery required. The lady broke down & began sobbing inconsolably, and Rhea pretended to care even though she had no time for such emotions because she believed in not getting emotionally attached to patients.

"She needs to undergo the surgery as soon as possible," Rhea said, turning to the husband, whom she believed to be more sensible even though he was distraught by the news.

As much as Rhea was eager to operate on the lady to meet the targets set by the MD, the truth was that the woman required surgery to take out the disease and prevent its spread as well.

"Has the disease spread?" the husband asked, leaning forward with arms crossed across his chest.

It was a genuine question, and one Rhea was used to answering.

"The CT scan does not show any spread. But I can accurately assess it only after I have opened her up and seen it for myself," she said, brushing off a few strands of stray hair from her face.

Rhea had seen enough cases where the CT scans had shown that there was no spread of disease, only to be proven wrong during the surgery.

"In your experience, what is the hope of my wife being perfectly normal following the surgery?" asked the husband.

This was a tricky question. If there was no spread and the surgery was performed adequately, the chances of the patient doing well were extremely high. At the same time, the prognosis was guarded if there was spread to the liver or other sites. She explained the same to them.

They were quiet for a while, trying to process all the information they had just been bombarded with. She knew that accepting the fact that one had cancer was hard, and so she didn't want to rush them. But at the same time, she wished they made up their minds fast for the patient's and Rhea's sake.

"How much will the treatment cost, doctor?" asked the husband.

She was accustomed to this question and had fine-tuned her answers. If the surgery was performed at another hospital, it would cost around two lakhs.

"The surgery will cost around five lakhs, and if she requires chemotherapy post-surgery, it will add to the cost. Of course, you can get the surgery done elsewhere for much less, but I can't vouch for the facilities and expertise available there," said Rhea.

She could see the indecision on the husband's face. On the one hand, Rhea had assured him that he would not get a better facility than the one at White Arc, but on the other hand, the price was steep as well.

"Do you have medical insurance?" she asked him, hoping that would make matters much easier for both of them.

"No, we don't. But I'll arrange the money somehow," he said, holding his wife's hand.

Rhea stared at the couple. She imagined they had kids in high school and wondered how they would break the news to them. Once they did, how would the kids react? She also wondered how they would arrange the money for the treatment. *Would he have to sell some of his belongings? Will he mortgage his house?* But she didn't want to know the answers to these questions because she had hardwired herself not to get into personal details besides the patient's treatment.

"Can I ask you something, if you don't mind, doctor?" asked the husband.

"Of course!" said Rhea. "I want you to clarify all doubts before committing to the surgery."

"Since my wife's life is at stake here, I just wanted to know how many years of experience you have performing these kinds of surgeries," he asked.

Rhea was taken aback by the question because she

expected him to ask her something about the surgery rather than her experience. Of course, she was more than capable of performing the surgery, for that matter, any surgery, thanks to the high-volume institutions she had studied in. However, when asked to summarise her experience in terms of the years she has worked there, she would fall way short of the seniors in her department.

"I have more than enough experience dealing with these cases, and the proof is all here," she said, pointing to the wall behind her that displayed her various degrees.

It came out more discourteously than she intended, but she didn't care. She couldn't stand it when someone questioned her ability based on her youthful appearance or her gender. She remembered her non-medical friend teasing her, saying patients can never take a young, attractive female doctor seriously. When Rhea looked at the husband's face, she could see that her answer had not convinced him. He wanted to hear a specific number, but she refused to give him one. There was an uncomfortable silence in the room, and Rhea noticed the nurse, who was privy to the conversation, shift uncomfortably beside her.

"We'll go home, discuss with our family, and get back to you," he said, trying to sound courteous, but she could sense the change in the tone of his voice.

Rhea nodded without saying a word because she knew she would not see them again. They rose from their seats, escorted to the door by the nurse, with the wife still sobbing. Rhea watched them leave, unable to decide whether she was angry or felt sorry for them. She waited for the nurse to usher in the next patient, but the nurse seemed rooted to the ground, peering out of the door with her back to Rhea.

"What are you doing?" Rhea demanded.

The nurse turned around at once as if she had been jolted.

"I am sorry, ma'am," she said as she looked outside for the next patient.

"What were you looking at?" Rhea asked curiously.

The nurse hesitated a bit, which fuelled Rhea's curiosity even more. She shifted uncomfortably in front of the door, twirling the side of her white skirt with the fingers of her right hand like a schoolgirl caught doing something wrong.

"I was just trying to see where the previous patient went, ma'am," she whispered.

"Where did they go?" Rhea asked, even though she had already guessed the answer.

"They went to the opposite cabin, madam," she said, shifting her gaze to the floor.

That was the cabin of one of the senior consultants. Rhea clutched the armrest of her chair until her knuckles turned white, reigning in her anger while her face remained impassive. She no longer felt sorry for the couple.

#

The pattern continued over the next few days. Though she was seeing quite a few patients in the outpatient department, none of them were converting into surgeries. Either the patients didn't require surgeries, or the ones who did didn't return to her. It was as if her meeting with the MD had jinxed her and induced a dry spell. She knew that if the same continued, they would soon show her the door.

"Why are there no operable cases?" she asked the nurse.

It was more as if Rhea was thinking aloud. The nurse, whom Rhea rarely spoke to unless she needed something, jumped at this unusual question from her boss.

"Probably because it is exam season for the school-going children, madam," she said, rising from the stool on which she was seated in the corner of the room. "Most people defer visiting the doctors during exam season."

Being single, Rhea was unaware of such a phenomenon and found it mindless. *If you are sick, you visit the doctor. You don't wait for some stupid exams of your kids to finish.*

"What about the other consultants? Are they operating cases?" asked Rhea.

"Yes, madam. They operate at least one case every day, sometimes even two or three," replied the nurse, privy to all the gossip from her fellow nurses.

The news stung Rhea more sharply than it should have. *How could there be so much disparity between consultants of the same department in the same hospital?* It was both absurd and humiliating. She knew she could not let it continue like this and had to do something to *level up,* as the MD had put it. *But what could she do to get out of this rut?* She knew of her batch mates who had hired experts to develop websites showcasing their work. Some of them had their own YouTube channels where they uploaded videos of their surgeries, generating many viewers that translated into patients. Some advertised themselves on TV and in newspapers with ads that cost a fortune. She had even heard of doctors promoting themselves on Facebook and Instagram. So far, she had never indulged in these gimmicks since she believed that her work should do the talking and had no interest or time for social media sites. She didn't even have a social media account.

Just then, there was a knock at the door, and a family of three peered in through the half-open door.

"May we come in, doctor?" asked the tall, skinny, middle-aged, bespectacled man who looked like the father.

"Please do," replied Rhea as the nurse ushered them in and seated them on the chairs in front of Rhea.

"Doctor, our son has been complaining of stomach pain for the past few days," said the mother, pointing to the boy sitting between them.

The boy appeared to be around 15 years old and had a wiry build like his father. His hair was bushy, curly, and dishevelled, and he hadn't seen a barber in a long time. He also had dark circles under his eyes and appeared to be sleep-deprived. Rhea asked the boy a series of questions and discovered that he was preparing for his exams, studying for long hours, eating irregularly, and drinking lots of coffee to stay awake, which explained his appearance. He had recently started experiencing stomach pain, mainly when he hadn't eaten.

Rhea asked him to lie on the examination table in the corner of the room. She examined him thoroughly and found nothing wrong except for gastritis.

As she was walking back to her chair, out of nowhere, the MD's voice echoed in her ears: *Do something, by fair means or foul.* The voice sounded so real that she turned to see if he was beside her. When he said it, he didn't have to spell out to her what he meant because Rhea understood perfectly. It had been a week since that conversation with him, and in that time, she had not operated a single case while her colleagues were wielding their scalpels every day.

"I think he has appendicitis," she said, looking at the parents.

She didn't know how the lie had come out of her lips so spontaneously; it was the first lie she had ever told her patients. It felt weird the moment the words escaped her lips. Once the words were spoken, there was no way of taking them back. She saw the look of terror in the mother's eyes and noticed the creases on the father's forehead deepen with worry.

"We'll do a scan and a couple of blood tests and take it from there," she said, hoping they would not detect the quiver in her voice.

The parents seemed too dazed to understand what was happening. They quietly accepted the scan and blood forms and walked to the radiology department, escorted by the nurse.

When they left her cabin, Rhea picked up her phone and dialled the number of the hospital's radiologist, who was her junior during MBBS.

"Good morning, Dr Rhea," said the radiologist. "What can I do for you?"

"I needed a favour," she said. "I have just sent a 15-year-old boy to you. I want you to give him a report of acute appendicitis," she said with her eyes closed.

Chapter Three

After a refreshing shower that washed away all the tiredness of her day, Rhea walked into the brightly lit dining room in her pink pyjamas with a pink towel wrapped around her hair. The tantalizing aroma of dinner prepared by her mother greeted her. Her parents were already seated at the table. Her brother Rahul was there too, dressed in a black vest and red shorts, but he was too busy tapping his phone screen to notice Rhea's arrival. Their empty plates showed that they were waiting for her to begin. She had berated them several times not to wait for her, but it was useless because her father would say that she was never at home and they would all like to have dinner together when she was. *A family that eats together stays together*. That was her father's mantra during her childhood, and there was never a meal that all four of them had not eaten together back then. It was a ritual they had followed strictly until she became a doctor. The hectic schedules made it impossible for her to be present at every meal, and often, she would eat cold food alone late at night, straight out of the fridge when the rest of the family was fast asleep.

"How was your day?" asked her father as she sat beside him.

Manoj Sharma, Rhea's father, was a well-built man in his early sixties. He had thick salt-and-pepper hair and always dressed in white Kurtas and pyjamas, even at home. He was a retired maths professor at a pre-university college where he taught for 30 years and was highly respected by his colleagues and students. He took great pride in his children's accomplishments, but it was evident to everyone that Rhea held a special place in his heart.

Just as Rhea was about to answer his question, Rahul cursed aloud, looking at his phone screen. Their mother said a silent prayer as if to cleanse herself for hearing the cuss word and probably to cleanse her son as well. Rhea didn't know what was wrong but inwardly chuckled at their theatrics.

"What happened, son?" asked their concerned mother.

Rhea's mother was a plump, rotund woman who seemed to forever be in a hurry, though she was going nowhere. She was always dressed in colourful nighties that were too bright for Rhea's taste. Though she was just a couple of years younger than their father, she did not have a single grey hair on her head, a gift Rhea hoped to inherit someday. She was a homemaker and had dedicated her life to the three of them. But Rhea always joked that Rahul was to their mother what Rhea was to their father. Rahul seemed to be the whole and soul of their mother's existence. It didn't help that Rhea and her mother always seemed to have a clash of ideologies ever since she was a child, leading to confrontations and arguments between the two that continued even to this day.

"Everything, Mom," he said, still staring at his phone, which was held in his left hand. He scooped rice from the bowl onto his plate with his right hand without bothering about the rest of them.

"You are not ill, right?" her mother asked, touching his forehead with the back of her hand.

"For heaven's sake, Mom! He is 27 years old. Stop

treating him like a baby." Rhea said with a look of disgust.

"Jealous, much?" asked Rahul, smiling, taking his eyes off the phone for the first time since she arrived.

"Jealous?" countered Rhea. "I feel you are pathetic. But I am proud to say you are not one of those independent, macho men out there. You are exactly how those men imagine women to be," she added sarcastically, never letting go of an opportunity to take a swipe at men who considered themselves superior to women.

"So you are trying to tell me you are proud of me," replied Rahul, smirking.

Everyone except their mother laughed, and they began their meal.

"So what's the big problem?" asked Rhea after they had eaten a few morsels.

Rhea always marvelled at two things about her mother. One was her fantastic cooking skills, and the other was her ability to remind Rhea of being unmarried at 33, irrespective of the discussion. That was their most recent clash of ideologies.

"It's my job," Rahul said disgustedly with a mouth full of rice. "After my campus interview, they told me they wanted me to join work in the first week of April. Today, they called me out of nowhere and said I must join in the 2nd week of February."

Rhea stopped eating and looked up at him in mock disgust. It was the last week of January, and he still had two weeks to join. Rahul was an outstanding student like her, who had done computer science engineering at IIT, Madras. After topping in almost all his subjects in his course, he had bagged a dream job at Facebook through campus recruitment and was offered a pay package that even dwarfed Rhea's. When she was 27, she remembered that she was still studying and living off a measly stipend, and he was cribbing about joining Facebook.

Rahul looked at Rhea and knew what she was thinking. He flung a few morsels of rice on her, and she slapped him on his arm. According to her, he was the most immature 27-year-old.

"It's not that I don't want to join. The issue is that I had booked tickets to Leh Ladakh for two weeks in February, and now neither will I get to go nor will I get a refund," he said, shaking his head disappointedly.

Rahul loved backpacking through different places and had already seen half of the country. Every four to five months, he would pack his bags in search of a trekking destination within India, alone or with his friends. He preferred to go on treks and bike rides to remote locations rather than attend parties like boys his age usually did. On the other hand, she had neither any interest in parties nor seen the world outside her hostels in Mumbai and Pune.

"I can't believe you consider a silly trip more important than a prestigious job," said Rhea.

"Nerds like you will never understand the exhilarating feeling of venturing on an outdoor trip through the rough terrain with the cool breeze hitting your face underneath the blanket of stars at night," said Rahul poetically.

Rhea pinched him on his arm, and he swatted her arm away. Their mother scolded both of them while their father only laughed. They continued with their meal in silence.

"How come Her Highness is home for dinner today? Did they fire you?" Rahul asked.

Considering the events of the past couple of weeks, the comment stung more than it should have, though Rhea knew it was made in jest. She glared at him, but it didn't affect him since he continued grinning at her.

"Things are a little dull at the hospital," she said.

"Must be because of the exam season," her father offered support as always.

Everyone knows about the stupid exam season phenomenon except me, thought Rhea.

"Did you perform any interesting surgeries today?" Rahul asked.

He had always disliked medicine and was scared of hospitals. However, he found joy in listening to the exciting cases she operated on, especially the bloody and gory ones that involved stab injuries, as he was a fan of crime shows. Despite having annoyed her since childhood, Rhea knew he cherished and respected her. She suggested he pursue a medical career, but he declined and chose engineering. Rhea would occasionally tease him, saying that if he had become a doctor, all the nurses in the hospital would have been smitten with him, given his tall, muscular build, curly hair, and dreamy eyes.

"Just a routine appendicectomy," said Rhea

"Was it gruesome?" asked Rahul, his interest peaking.

"Nothing out of the ordinary. A 15-year-old boy. The surgery went well, so he'll do well." Rhea said, shifting uncomfortably in her chair without looking up from her plate.

"15-year-old boy?" asked Rahul. "Doesn't he have exams?"

"Yes, he does. But an emergency surgery cannot wait for exams," replied Rhea, not wanting to discuss it.

It was precisely what she had told the parents when they had come back to her cabin from the radiology department with the report of acute appendicitis, a report her friend had doctored at her request.

"What should we do now, doctor?" the concerned father of the boy had asked her.

"He will require emergency surgery today itself," Rhea replied without a hint of remorse in her voice.

"Can the surgery wait? He is the class topper, and if he doesn't attend the exam, not only will he lose out on his rank, he will also lose a year," said the mother in tears as if she had been diagnosed with cancer and had only one day to live.

"We can delay the surgery, but if the appendix ruptures, then it is a life-threatening condition," replied Rhea, which was true except for the fact that the boy wasn't suffering from appendicitis.

She could see the dilemma on each of their faces. On the one hand, all three were worried about losing out on a year if the boy didn't answer his exams. But they also knew that his life was at risk if they didn't go ahead with the surgery.

"We'll get the surgery done," said the father emphatically without even discussing it with his wife and the son.

Rhea was taken aback by the abruptness of his decision since she thought they would need much more convincing.

"Do you need some time to discuss this as a family outside?" she asked them, even though his decision overjoyed her.

"What is the need for discussion, doctor?" said the father kindly. "You are our doctor. I don't trust anyone more than a doctor. So, if you say that it is a life-threatening condition, then we will go ahead with the surgery since we don't want to take any chances with our son's health. Exams will come and go, but our son is more important."

If Rhea had been affected by such deep devotion of a patient, she would probably have backed out of the surgery herself. However, she had no emotional connection with her patients, so his words did not make any impression. All she cared about was that they had agreed to the surgery. She immediately instructed the nurse to get the necessary procedures for admission done while she explained the surgery process and took the consent associated with it from the parents. The surgery was posted within two hours because Rhea didn't want to risk the parents changing their minds.

Two hours later, Rhea saw a perfectly normal appendix when she opened the abdomen. Before disconnecting it, she had crushed it multiple times with a pair of forceps so that the pathologist would report it as a case of an inflamed appendix.

#

After dinner, Rhea sat on the long, grey, upholstered living room sofa with her legs on the coffee table. She was surfing through the TV channels without actually watching any of them. She also kept checking her phone for any emergency cases from the hospital, even though the phone was set to ringing mode. Her father sat on the lounge chair beside her, quietly observing the changing TV channels as if watching the most exciting program. Rhea glanced at him and smiled, reflecting on how patient he had been with her over the years, especially when she would become difficult to manage. He was her biggest supporter, always encouraging her to pursue her dreams and forgiving her for all her childhood mistakes. He was the only man she had ever respected in her life. She wondered what he would say if she told him the truth about the boy she had operated on that evening. However, the thought made her uncomfortable, and she brushed it aside.

Rahul plopped himself on the same sofa as her, placing his head on the opposite end and his feet on her lap. He was still furiously tapping away on his phone. Rhea pushed his feet off her, but he put them back on her. She wondered why and whom he would message all day when it was much easier to call and speak instead. That's when she remembered something that was on her mind that morning.

"Can you create a Facebook account for me?" she asked Rahul, removing the towel from her head and letting her brown hair swoop down her shoulders.

"Why?" asked Rahul without looking up from his phone.

Rhea didn't want to tell him she wanted to use it to advertise herself because he would tease her if she did so.

"Why not?" asked Rhea. "Everyone seems to be on Facebook, and it would be weird for me not to have one when my brother is going to be working for them."

Rahul grinned, showing he was convinced. He rose and sat beside her, picking up her phone and using it to download the app.

"Why don't you create an account on Shaadi.com simultaneously," said her mother, swooping into the room out of nowhere with a half-washed plate in her hands.

Rahul chuckled while Rhea ignored her mother and watched her brother create her Facebook account. There was a full minute's silence in the room except for the news anchor on TV, the channel Rhea had unintentionally stopped on.

"For how long will you ignore me regarding this? You are 33 years old. Girls your age are mothers of two kids. Work is not everything. It would be best if you also had a companion in life," her mother said.

Rhea had been hearing the same lecture for the past

five years, especially after her mother returned from any wedding function. Her mother seemed obsessed with her marriage, and it infuriated Rhea. She belittled all that Rhea had achieved in her career just because she wasn't married with kids yet. Rhea was under a lot of pressure at work right now, and the last thing she wanted was to think about marriage. Taking care of a husband and kids seemed unimaginable to her.

"I don't need a marriage website to find me a boy. I think I am educated enough and good-looking enough for boys to ask for my hand anyway," replied Rhea sternly.

"Oh, is it? Then where are those boys?" demanded her mother, flailing her arms and sprinkling soapy droplets on them from the half-washed plate. "You think you will get married easily because you are a doctor? Boys don't want girls who wear pants and suits."

"If you could find a husband, surely I will find one too," replied Rhea.

It was a spontaneous response. Something Rhea was known for. She could not resist giving back to someone, even if it were her mother. If someone was wrong, she had to put them in place.

"Did you hear how she speaks to her mother?" her mother said, turning towards their father.

"Let her be Savita. She is just beginning her career and needs more time," replied her father reassuringly. "And her comment was more an insult to me than you, I think," he added with a smirk.

Rhea and Rahul burst out laughing, which infuriated their mother even more.

"Both father and daughter and cut from the same loom of cloth," she said and stormed out of the room.

Rhea looked at her father and smiled. He grinned mischievously. Nothing in the world was more important to him than her. She hoped to make him proud someday, even though she knew he was already proud of her achievements.

"Your account is done," said Rahul, showing her phone. He then gave her a full tour of her Facebook profile.

Chapter Four

The next day, things seemed to have taken a turn for the better. While the number of patients visiting her outpatient department was slimmer than usual, Rhea had better luck with the number of admissions. By afternoon, she had admitted two patients: a patient diagnosed to have a hiatus hernia, a pathology associated with the esophagus. She planned to operate on him the very next day. The other was a patient who complained of bleeding while passing stools and whom Rhea, after examination, suspected to have cancer of the rectum and planned to complete the necessary investigations so she could operate on him within the next couple of days.

At lunchtime, the nurse strolled into the cabin, beaming from ear to ear.

"Why are you so happy?" Rhea asked, packing her red bag to go out for lunch.

"Today, we have more admissions so far than the other two consultants, madam," she said, smiling as if she was the one who would operate on them.

Rhea couldn't help but smile at her enthusiasm. The young nurse had been posted with her ever since she joined White Arc three years ago, fresh out of nursing school. Though Rhea had found her clumsy at first and not up to the standards Rhea demanded, she had improved over time. She was petite, with eager eyes and a dark complexion. She tried her best to impress Rhea, but that was no mean task. Rhea hardly spoke to her except for barking orders at her or scolding her.

"Good," said Rhea with no overt display of friendliness.

"I am thrilled, madam," continued the nurse, "You are a great surgeon, and I look up to you. I couldn't imagine assisting someone else if you left."

The moment the words left her mouth, the nurse bit her lips. In her enthusiasm to impress her boss, she had revealed more than she intended. Rhea stopped combing her hair with a brush she had just pulled out of her handbag and glared at her with narrowed eyes.

"Who told you I was leaving?" she asked, her smile suddenly vanishing.

The nurse didn't know where to look or what to say, and her eyes ran roughshod all over the place. Nobody knew more about Rhea's temper than her.

"I asked you, who told you I was leaving?" she said again slowly and deliberately as if she were talking to a 5-year-old, the rage palpable in her voice.

"Some nurses said that the management has given you an ultimatum to increase your patient count or leave, madam," she said.

"You little scum," Rhea said in her usual cold tone. "You are not even good at what you are supposed to do, and you and your fellow pathetic nurses are passing judgements about my work? Who the hell do you think you are?"

The nurse who was beaming just a few minutes ago broke down completely, with tears flowing unabated, which satisfied Rhea. She couldn't believe that her job had become a topic of gossip for the nurses and other lowly hospital staff. She wondered who could have leaked the information that only the MD and she were privy to. She huffed out of the cabin, leaving behind the sobbing nurse.

#

When Rhea returned to the cabin after lunch, she found the nurse already sitting on a stool in the corner. The nurse's eyes were swollen and red as if she had been crying. Upon seeing Rhea, the nurse stood up immediately, but Rhea ignored her and walked to the hangar to put on her apron. Once she had donned her apron over her brown pantsuit, she sat behind her desk.

"Send in the next patient," she instructed sternly.

"There are no appointments for this afternoon, madam. But I will go out and look for new patients," said the nurse, dabbing her eyes with her handkerchief, eager to impress Rhea.

Rhea watched the nurse leave and felt relieved to have some time alone. She didn't want to look at the nurse's face anymore. Rhea felt disgusted and betrayed that people were gossiping about her job security. She was sure that some of them would even place bets on whether she would keep her job. This kind of mentality was one of the reasons why Rhea avoided socializing with others in the hospital. She had no friends there because she had never gone out of her way to please anyone. All she cared about was her work, which she did diligently, and nothing else mattered.

As she had nothing else to do, Rhea decided to explore the newly installed Facebook app on her phone. Upon opening the app, she was surprised to find several friend requests from people she had not met in a long time. Some were her MBBS batchmates, but what caught her off guard were the friend requests from her schoolmates. She could hardly recognize many of them from their present pictures as they had changed so much over the years. Rhea was never one to keep in touch

30

with friends, and she found the entire process of meeting friends tiresome. It had been years since she had been out for dinner with anyone or even had a conversation with someone for a considerable length of time unless it was work-related. She did not understand why people spoke for hours on the phone.

The thought of phone conversations reminded her that she had not been informed of the blood reports of the two patients she had admitted that morning. It was the norm for the ward nurse to inform all the blood reports within a few hours of a patient's admission. She picked up the landline beside her, connected to the 4th-floor counter, and immediately admonished the nurse who picked up the call for not having informed her about the patients.

"But there are no admissions for you so far, madam," replied the terrified ward nurse on the phone.

"Don't talk nonsense," yelled Rhea. "I have written the admission files myself."

Rhea heard rapid conversations in hushed voices on the other side of the phone as the nurses scrambled to find out about the missing patients.

"Sorry, madam. We didn't get any admissions from you today. There were just two patients admitted by Dr. Nathwani," the nurse replied after a few minutes of hunting down the patients.

Dr Ishwar Nathwani was the senior consultant in the department. *That is odd,* thought Rhea. Where could her patients have disappeared? She hung up and called the registration desk to find out if her patients had been admitted to some other ward, but the receptionist confirmed that there were indeed no patients admitted under her that day.

She wondered what had happened to her patients.

Sometimes, patients preferred to have lunch at home before getting admitted. Or maybe they had returned home to pack their bags and make the necessary arrangements before coming to the hospital. Rhea hoped both patients would arrive soon, especially the one with a hiatus hernia. She couldn't operate on him the next day if he arrived too late.

Rhea sat in her cabin until 6 PM. There were only a few new consultations after lunch. What made it worse was that the two patients whom she had admitted that morning never arrived, which meant that she had no surgeries posted for the next day. Never before had she suffered such a dry spell in the hospital, and it couldn't have come at a worse time for her.

#

The following day, Rhea was strutting towards her cabin in her beige pantsuit and brown stilettos through the hospital lobby; she glanced at the second floor, where an elderly lady was leaning against the railing. When the woman turned to face Rhea, she recognized her to be the wife of the patient with the hiatus hernia, who was supposed to be operated on by her that day but had never turned up. Rhea stopped in her tracks, locked eyes with the woman, and could see the look of uncertainty on her face as if she was caught doing something wrong.

Rhea changed her course and trudged up the stairs to the second floor, where the slightly stooped lady with silvery hair like her father and a wrinkled face stood with fear in her eyes in a dark maroon saree.

"I waited for you guys till late last evening," Rhea told her without bothering to make small talk. "How come you didn't get admitted?"

The lady squirmed as if trying to conjure up the words

but couldn't find them. Rhea knew at once that there was something wrong.

"My husband is in surgery right now," the lady whispered.

It took Rhea a moment to figure out what was going on. It then struck her that they were on the second floor, outside the OT complex. It was obvious that her husband was in surgery; why else would she be standing there?

"Who is operating on your husband?" she asked calmly.

"Dr Ishwar Nathwani," replied the lady.

Rhea's mind was in turmoil, although she nodded absentmindedly. She initially felt like confronting the lady but decided against it since they were outside the operating room complex where her husband was undergoing surgery, and there were several people around. She didn't want to risk damaging the hospital's or her reputation by berating the patient's relative in public. So, she restrained herself and started walking towards the stairs. However, just as she reached the corner, she turned around.

"Can I ask you something?" asked Rhea. "Why did you choose Dr Nathwani over me?"

She knew the lady would tell her he was far more experienced than her, but she still wanted to hear it from her.

"The gentleman at the *help desk* informed us that Dr Nathwani was more experienced and better qualified to operate on my husband than you. I am very sorry," she said with a genuine look of apology.

"Which gentleman are you talking about?" asked Rhea, confused.

From their vantage point on the 2nd floor, the lady pointed down below at the lobby to the person sitting alone beside the entrance at the small help desk in a tieless black suit, white shirt, and hospital ID card slung around his neck. Rhea's head was spinning. *Who was this guy, and why was he diverting my patients to Dr Nathwani?*

Rhea realized something was fishy. She hurried up the stairs to the fourth floor, where her department's patients were admitted. The clacking of her heels along the corridors was enough for the nurses to know she was approaching, and all four stood up before she arrived.

"Show me the files of the two patients admitted under Dr Nathwani yesterday," she ordered.

The nurses ran helter-skelter, rummaging through the mountain of files at the counter.

"One of them is in surgery, madam," offered one nurse.

"I know," replied Rhea. "Show me the other one."

The nurse presented the blue file, and sure enough, the name on it was the same as that of the one she had seen in her cabin the previous day.

"Which room?" Rhea demanded.

"321," replied the nurse.

Before the nurse could react, Rhea walked straight towards the room. The confused nurses hurried behind her with the file in hand. When she arrived at room 321, Rhea pushed open the door and walked in without knocking. On seeing her, both the patient lying on the bed in a hospital gown and his wife on the chair stood up.

"I just want to know one thing," Rhea said, "Why did you change your doctor?"

"The gentleman at the help desk…" began the patient, but before he could complete his sentence, Rhea was out of the door because she had gotten the answer she had come for.

Rhea hurried down the stairs, feeling her blood pumping rapidly through her veins. As she reached the ground floor, she walked through a crowd of patients towards the help desk near the entrance. The young man seated there was in his early twenties with short, spiked hair and a clean-shaven face. Rhea hadn't paid attention to who sat at the help desk for the past three years as it didn't concern her. However, when the young man saw Rhea approaching him, the look of fear on his face convinced her about her doubts.

"Who the hell are you to divert my patients to other consultants?" she screamed, pointing a finger at him when she arrived at the desk.

Everyone at the registration counter, the employees, the patients, the relatives, and even the security personnel at the entrance stopped what they were doing and looked at them, but she didn't care.

The boy at the help desk froze under Rhea's intimidating gaze. The mad rage on her face was enough for him to know that this was no ordinary woman and she could shred him to pieces.

"Madam, I am sorry," he whispered, standing up.

"To hell with your apology," screamed Rhea. "I will report you to the authorities and then chop off your head in front of them."

The boy was shivering with fear now. He stood mute, looking at the ground, which infuriated Rhea even more.

She walked towards him, placed her hands on the desk, and leaned forward until her face was inches away from his.

"I am asking you one last time," she said in a low, slow, cold voice, as she always did when enraged. "Why did you divert two of my patients to Dr Nathwani?"

It was too much for the boy to take, and he knew there was no other way than to tell Rhea the truth.

"Dr Nathwani paid me to do so," he whispered, leaving Rhea's mouth agape.

Chapter Five

Rhea sat heavily in her cabin chair; her head cradled in her hands as she faced the desk with her eyes closed. After confronting the help desk personnel, she sent the nurse away so she could have time to think and make sense of everything.

The information she had just received was hard to digest. *How could a senior consultant of Dr. Nathwani's calibre stoop to such a low level?* She was almost thirty years his junior, yet he found it necessary to divert her patients to him by paying someone. *Am I that big a threat to him?* And if he felt so, Rhea couldn't help but be inwardly proud that it had driven him to do something sinister like what he had done.

But it still didn't douse Rhea's anger or take away her sense of betrayal about the whole affair. She perceived that the best course of action would be for her to confront Dr Nathwani. Rhea was not someone to stay stifled in the face of injustice, and she also wanted to know if the boy at the help desk was lying, though she could not think of any reason for him to do so. She composed herself for a few minutes and decided to speak to Dr Nathwani. She stood up, smoothened her beige suit with her hands and walked out of her cabin towards his through scores of patients in the waiting area. His cabin was just a few steps away across the hall, opposite hers.

When she reached his closed door, with his credentials embossed on a golden plate in black letters, she knocked on it, turned the knob, pushed the door slightly, and peeped in. To her luck, the patient inside was standing up to leave.

"May I talk to you for a minute, sir?" Rhea asked, standing at the door.

She did not miss the look of surprise on his face, but to his credit, Dr Nathwani recovered instantly.

"Yes, of course. Please take a seat," he said politely, pointing to the chair the patient had vacated.

Rhea took a seat and scrutinized him. Her heart was pounding; she was uncertain if it was out of anger or anxiety. She was about to accuse one of the hospital's senior consultants of jeopardizing her practice, which caused even someone as strong as Rhea to be nervous. Dr Nathwani appeared composed in his perfectly fitting black suit. He was a tall, slightly overweight man, towering over Rhea even when seated. He was fair-skinned, and his face was lined with wrinkles that spoke of wisdom accumulated from 30 years of experience in the field of surgery. There was a slight stoop to his frame, something many surgeons his age suffered thanks to hours of bending and operating on patients. Sparse salt and pepper hair covered his head, which he had oiled in place.

"What can I do for you, Dr Rhea?" he said, adjusting his rimless spectacles.

Rhea bit her lip as she didn't know how to begin the conversation. If he were her subordinate, she would have bitten his head off by now. But he was a well-respected, well-known senior consultant at the hospital and the city.

"Sir, two of your patients have been admitted under your care," she said, choosing her words carefully.

He didn't flinch—it was as if he were made of stone. He leaned back in his chair, his gaze fixed on her, and for an instant, Rhea felt as if she was the one who had done something wrong. She waited for a response, but he seemed to be taking his sweet time.

"And?" he asked, finally breaking the uncomfortable silence.

Rhea's mind was abuzz, and she wondered how best she could put her thoughts into words.

"I just found out that the guy at the help desk diverted those patients to you, sir," she said, careful not to accuse him of anything.

"Is that so?" he asked, leaning forward, placing his elbows on the table and clasping his palms together. "And how did he do it?"

Rhea noted that Dr Nathwani wasn't surprised by the information, nor did he deny it.

"He told them I was less experienced and not as good as you, sir," replied Rhea, slowly losing her calm since she knew she was being toyed with.

"And what is wrong with that? It's the truth, isn't it?" he said, leaning back on his chair and gently swivelling it side to side, his gaze on Rhea.

Rhea couldn't believe the man's audacity. Not only was he not taken aback by the revelation, but he was defending it. She had come to him, trying to be as reasonable and subdued as possible, which was unlike her, but he was taking advantage of her submissiveness.

"So you knew about it?" she said, raising her voice slightly. "Is it true you paid him to do so?"

Dr Nathwani guffawed. It was as if he was enjoying the little showdown as much as she hated it.

"I neither deny nor accept anything, Dr. Rhea. What matters is that the patients believed him."

Rhea had heard enough. Whatever little patience she

possessed was spent. She stood up and slapped the top of the table with both her hands in anger as she could no longer play the stupid game.

"How can a man of your stature stoop so low, Dr Nathwani?" she said through clenched teeth.

Dr. Nathwani remained stoic. He also didn't fail to notice that she had stopped addressing him as *sir*.

"Please sit down, Dr. Rhea," he said without raising his voice. "And don't you dare cross the line with me?"

"You are the one crossing the line, Dr. Nathwani," spat out Rhea, still standing. Wait until I inform the board about your behaviour."

Dr Nathwani laughed aloud. This time, it was a hearty laugh.

"And what exactly are you going to tell them, Dr. Rhea?" he asked with a smile. "That I, Dr. Ishwar Nathwani, the senior consultant at White Arc, one of the most well-respected surgeons in the state who has been serving this hospital from its humble roots even before you entered high school, is stealing patients from you? Whom do you think they are going to believe?"

"I have proof," Rhea countered. "I will use the help desk boy and the patients as witnesses."

"The patients will say the boy advised them to switch doctors because of my superior experience. The boy will say he did it out of his own accord since he is a big fan of my surgical work. Both of which will not be contested by the board," he said with a smirk.

Rhea realized he was right. He was powerful enough to shut up the boy regarding money changing hands. But she didn't want to show her uncertainty to him, as that would have meant conceding defeat.

"Wait till you see what I do," she said, even though she didn't know what she had in mind.

She turned around and walked in a huff towards the door to leave.

"And what do you think will happen when I tell them you falsified a report and operated on a boy who didn't require surgery?" said Dr Nathwani just as she was about to open the door and leave.

Rhea froze, unable to believe what she was hearing. She stood rooted to the ground, hand on the doorknob for support. Her legs had turned to jelly, and she felt like she would collapse any time. *How in the world had he found out about it?* She turned slowly to face him, even though she didn't want to.

"You stroll in here, trying to take the high moral ground, accusing me of poaching your patients while you are faking reports and performing unnecessary surgeries. At least I operate on genuine patients. So, whom does that make a cheat, Dr. Rhea?"

Rhea stood in silence, unable to formulate a response.

"Do you know what the board would do if I told them about your misdemeanours, Dr. Rhea?" he repeated.

Rhea didn't have an answer.

"The same thing they would do if you told them about what I did. NOTHING! The medical profession is a business Dr Rhea, a highly competitive one at that. You want patients, I want patients, and even the board wants patients. They don't care how you do it if you don't get caught. And if you get caught, they will throw you under the bus and continue as if nothing happened," he said with an expressionless face.

By fair means or foul, the words of the MD reverberated in her ears.

"Dr Rhea, in this business, we adapt and do everything possible to stay ahead. The moment you stop, someone else will overtake you. And if you are not smart enough, you will not last long," he said.

Rhea listened to every word he said; strangely, it made sense. He had lasted long enough in the profession to know precisely what he was talking about. She was not so different from him after all. She was a go-getter and would not stop at anything to reach her goal. The only difference was that she was just a beginner in the game while he was a seasoned campaigner.

Rhea gave him one long look and left the room without saying anything.

#

Rhea splashed water on her face after she returned to her cabin, trying to wash away all the negativity from her. She looked at herself in the mirror to see if Dr Nathwani's words affected her appearance. The tapering cheekbones, amber eyes, dusky skin, and flowing dark brown hair were all the same, yet somehow she felt different. She had barged into Dr Nathwani's cabin to confront him over the fact that he was cheating her out of her patients. But after listening to him, she felt his words made sense. When she joined White Arc Hospital, fresh after completing her studies, her only ambition was to perform surgeries day and night and make a name for herself. Of course, over time, money became a driving force as well. If at all she had to acquire the longevity that Dr. Nathwani enjoyed or attain Dr. Subhash Gupta, the MD's position someday, she had to do whatever it took, even if it meant blurring the lines between black and white. And she realized she had inadvertently already begun doing so by operating on the boy who didn't need the surgery. Dr

Nathwani was right. *Who was she to accuse him of doing wrong when she had already walked down a similar path?* It was a man's world, and the only way to beat them was to play their game better than them.

She spent the rest of the day with renewed vigour, seeing patients in her cabin. Whenever she admitted a patient, she would ask the nurse to accompany them to the registration counter and then to the ward for fear that they would be side-tracked by Dr. Nathwani or the boy at the help desk. However, she didn't know if they would pull the same stunt again now that she was privy to their scheme, but she didn't want to take any chances.

That evening, she packed her handbag and took the elevator to the 4th floor, where she checked on her admitted patients, their blood reports, and their scans. When she was finished, she rode the elevator back to the ground floor and was just about to leave the hospital premises when her phone buzzed, and the screen flashed the name of the hospital emergency section.

"Good evening, Dr Rhea," said the voice on the other end of the phone. "We have a patient with a stab injury to the abdomen who has just arrived."

Before the person could say anything more, Rhea cut the call and dashed towards the emergency section, which was on the right wing of the hospital.

The moment she entered the emergency section, whose 20 beds were all occupied, she saw the commotion on the last bed with a doctor performing CPR on the patient by applying rhythmic pressure on his chest with his hands and nurses rushing IV fluids into him and Rhea at once knew the situation was bleak. The young emergency medicine specialist, who seemed to be injecting a shot of adrenaline into the patient, saw Rhea approaching.

"A 35-year-old male construction worker slipped and fell off the first floor and landed on a sharp object that pierced his abdomen. He has lost a lot of blood since it took them some time to get him here. Honestly, I don't think there's much we can do," he said in between barking orders and injecting the patient.

Rhea saw a nurse holding a dressing pad onto the abdomen of the patient to stop the bleeding, which was soaking wet. The monitors showed shallow blood pressure and a barely recordable pulse.

"I'll speak to his relatives; you keep him alive," ordered Rhea.

As she left the emergency room, security personnel directed her toward two women in the waiting area. The women were holding hands and crying in the corner. One was much older with gray hair and a stooped back, while the other was in her twenties. They wore old torn sarees that didn't quite fit in with the upscale White Arc hospital. A bearded middle-aged man stood a little away from them, dressed in a white shirt and trousers. He looked more affluent than the two women. When the security personnel told the group that Rhea was their doctor, they hurried over to her.

"Doctor, how is my son?" asked the older woman.

"Please save my husband," said the younger one, who knew the situation was grave.

"I won't lie to you, but there seems to be little hope," Rhea explained the patient's condition, and both broke down completely.

Hearing this, the gentleman in white ushered Rhea to the corner of the waiting area, away from the two sobbing women.

"I am his employer, doctor," whispered the man with a worried look. "If something happens to him, I will have to suffer a huge backlash since I am required to insure all my employees, which I haven't done. So I pray to you to save him; I will pay the expenses no matter how much it costs."

Upon hearing the words, Rhea's mind went into overdrive. The cost was not a concern, as the low-income family would not have to pay a single penny, regardless of the final bill. She was free to try anything to save the patient. After all, the employer was responsible for not providing adequate safety equipment and deserved to cover all the expenses.

"We'll take him in for emergency surgery and do whatever is possible," she declared to all three of them, and the mother and wife's faces brightened with hope.

Rhea hurried back into the casualty to see that the commotion had subsided and the doctors and nurses were standing by the patient doing nothing.

"We lost him," declared the emergency medicine specialist with slumped shoulders to Rhea.

Rhea looked up at the monitor and saw that the BP and pulse rate were not recordable. However, the ECG monitor showed faint spikes due to the effect of the adrenaline infused into the patient, which would soon wear off, and the line would become flat.

"Give him another shot of adrenaline, rush another bottle of blood in, continue CPR, and shift him to the OT at once for emergency surgery," commanded Rhea.

"He's dead, doctor," said the young, bewildered emergency medicine specialist as if she had not understood him the first time.

"I am the surgeon here, doctor," said Rhea sternly to him. "He'll be dead when I say he is."

The air of finality and the tone of voice were enough for the EM specialist to back down. He injected the patient with another shot of adrenaline with the nurse performing CPR, and Rhea saw a few scattered spikes on the ECG monitor. She scampered to the OT on the 2nd floor to change into her scrubs while the patient was wheeled in.

#

The patient was lying on the OT table. Rhea scrubbed in for the case and stood with a scalpel in hand. She looked at the anaesthetist, who nodded, and she placed an incision on the abdomen of the patient.

#

The surgery took approximately an hour. Rhea had opened the abdomen and found that the spleen was the organ that had been pierced and was responsible for the massive bleeding. She dissected it and looked for any other organ injuries, of which there were none. She then clicked the pictures as proof of the nature of the injury and sutured the abdomen. The surgery was done well, and the patient was wheeled into the ICU, still on a ventilator.

The irony was that both Rhea and the anaesthetist knew the patient was dead before the surgery had begun.

Chapter Six

Rhea watched the mother bawl inconsolably while the wife passed out as some people around the ICU helped her to the chairs in the corner, where a nurse sprinkled water on her face. Rhea had just delivered the news of the death of the patient, having waited till the following day to let them feel like she had tried their best. She stood silently and watched as the nurses ushered the mother and the wife out of the ICU, having not only lost their son and husband but also the sole breadwinner of the family since the father was already dead. The employer of the deceased patient, who had promised to pay for the expenses of the treatment, approached Rhea.

"We tried our best," Rhea told the gentleman dressed in all white.

"Your best was not good enough, doctor. What good is a hospital like this if you can't save a patient's life?" he said bitterly.

Rhea was surprised by the sudden shift in his behaviour. Just the day before, he pleaded with her to do everything possible to save the patient so he would not be held liable for not providing his employees with the necessary safety equipment and insurance. However, now that the patient had died, his attitude had changed entirely. Rhea presumed that it was because he was now responsible for paying for the treatment of a deceased employee and was anticipating backlash from his workforce, which had led to the change in his demeanour.

"There is only so much we can do," said Rhea, not losing her cool after being in similar situations many times.

"We should probably have taken him to a place where they would have done better," he said, walking away.

Rhea wanted to call him out and give him an earful, but she chose against it because it would not have been the right time and place. Instead, she walked back to her cabin.

A few hours later, she was informed by the reception desk that all the formalities regarding the deceased patient had been completed. The bills had been paid, and they had released the body to them.

The rest of the day was uneventful.

#

Two days after the incident, Rhea received the biggest jolt of her life. In the morning, she was seated in her hospital cabin, waiting for her first patient of the day, when a young woman dressed in a black pantsuit similar to her entered her cabin. Her hair was tied in a bun, and she walked with her head held high as if she owned the place.

"Good morning, doctor," she said with a practiced smile.

"Good morning," replied Rhea. "How may I help you?"

"I needed to talk to you about something, doctor," she said, looking at the nurse and adding, "Alone."

There was something business-like about her appearance, confident and accusatory at the same time. Rhea felt uneasy immediately and knew that this was no ordinary consultation. She asked the nurse to leave the cabin.

"Yes?" replied Rhea once they were alone.

"I wanted to talk to you about a case you operated on a few days back," she said.

"Which one?" asked Rhea.

"The one that was brought dead," she replied sternly.

Rhea stiffened. It was like a bolt of lightning had struck her. *Who was this woman, and how did she know about this?*

"Excuse me? What are you talking about?" Rhea asked, even though she knew very well.

"I am a reporter from the FIRST NEWS channel, and we have evidence about the patient you operated on even though he was brought dead just so you could make money out of the family's misery," she said with a smug look.

"I don't care who you are; you have no right to accuse me of something like that without proof." Rhea countered, filled with unfathomable rage.

"We have all the proof in the world, doctor," she said condescendingly. "My purpose of this visit was merely to inform you that we will run this news on our channel tonight."

"Get out of here before I ask security to haul you out," screamed Rhea, standing up, unable to contain her anger.

The reporter stood up and quietly made her way to the door.

"You will pay for this dearly, Dr Rhea," she said in a low, chilly voice and exited the room.

#

By evening, all hell had broken loose around Rhea. As promised, The FIRST NEWS channel's headline read *SERIOUS MALPRACTICE IN A CORPORATE HOSPITAL.* Within no time, other local newspapers and news channels latched onto the news and swooped into the hospital premises with flashing cameras. The security personnel were having a hard time controlling the pandemonium.

Rhea watched the FIRST NEWS channel in her cabin all by herself.

"This is what the public gets for placing trust in doctors, especially in corporate hospitals," said the news anchor from her studio, looking straight into the camera as if she were talking to Rhea. She was the same lady who had visited Rhea that morning.

"A helpless family walks into White Arc hospital with one of their members in critical condition with the hope that the doctors to whom they accord God-like status would help them out. Instead, not only did they fail to save the patient, they delayed his treatment and then performed surgery on the dead patient to make a quick buck. This is the state of the medical profession today. How can these doctors live with themselves after committing such a heinous crime? We should bring them to justice," screamed the reporter, ending her lengthy monologue.

Rhea hurled abuses at the television set as if the reporter was right in front of her. The camera then panned away from the reporter to a gentleman dressed in all white seated beside her. The reporter introduced him as the patient's employer.

"Can you tell us exactly what happened that day, Mr. Bhaskar?" the reporter asked him, no doubt having rehearsed the entire conversation with him.

"My worker fell off the 2nd floor and sustained injuries to his abdomen when he landed on a sharp object. Within minutes, we shifted him to White Arc Hospital, where the doctors performed many manoeuvres on him instead of shifting him for surgery. Then, after quite some time, a surgeon came to us and asked us if the patient had insurance. I told her he didn't since I was still in the process of ensuring all my laborers, but I would pay the bill no matter how much it came up to. Within minutes, the patient was taken into surgery, and the very next morning, they declared him dead," said the gentleman with tears in his eyes.

Rhea couldn't believe what she was seeing on television. The employer had manipulated the story and was shedding crocodile tears. In reality, the patient had been brought to the hospital too late, and the White Arc Emergency team had done everything they could to save him. Rhea had never asked about the insurance, but the man had voluntarily confessed to not having insured his employees, even though he was supposed to.

"There you have it, folks," said the reporter, looking back at the camera. "What more evidence do you need?"

As if answering her question, the camera next moved to an old, run-down house, and the patient's wife and mother appeared on the screen in front of another reporter, wearing the same sarees they had on when they were at the hospital. The reporter bombarded the bewildered duo with more questions about what happened on that fateful day. Both narrated the incident teary-eyed, but unlike Mr. Bhaskar, they didn't manipulate the story.

"Do you think the doctors cheated you?" asked the reporter, thrusting the mic towards the mother.

"No," replied the mother. "The doctor was kind and tried her best to save my son."

The answer seemed to stun the reporter, who probably expected the mother to berate the doctors.

"Do you know your son was already dead when he

was wheeled into the operation theatre?" asked the reporter.

The turmoil on the mother's face was there for all to see. The reporter then asked her more questions, which seemed like she was shoving facts down the mother's throat to prove her point to the audience. At the end of it, the wife and mother were sobbing with the camera focused on them.

"This is the sorry image of what the doctors leave behind after a visit to the corrupt corporate hospitals," said the voice of the reporter behind the images.

Rhea switched off the television and held her head in her hands, unable to think clearly. *How could this have gone so wrong?* This had turned into a mess that would surely ruin her reputation. People were always looking for opportunities to put down doctors, and she knew no one would defend her. She only hoped that the management of White Arc would come to her aid and get her out of this mess since she had dedicated her life to the hospital, and their reputation was at stake, too.

At that very moment, her phone rang, and the secretary informed her that the MD, Dr. Gupta, wanted to speak with her in the boardroom.

#

Rhea was walking towards the elevator involuntarily as though an invisible force was pulling her. She was surrounded by patients, nurses, and hospital staff, but she avoided making eye contact, fearing that their faces would be full of judgment. Despite this, she didn't care much about their opinions, considering them as people who would achieve little in life and who envied her. She believed they would do anything to be in her position and, therefore, had no right to cast aspersions on her.

As she stepped out of the elevator on the sixth floor,

Rhea was greeted by calming music emanating from the invisible speakers. However, the music didn't have the desired effect on her today. The amber-tinged corridor was empty, and she wondered if she had misheard on the phone about the meeting location. With no other options, she proceeded towards the massive wooden boardroom door, placed her hand on the doorknob, turned it around, and walked inside for the first time.

The boardroom was a spacious chamber, but it was dimly lit, with only a few overhead lamps casting a faint light in the centre. The rest of the space was dark, and Rhea couldn't tell if it was always like that or if it was done on purpose to reflect the mood of the hospital. A rectangular mahogany table dominated the centre of the room, which seemed to be cut from the same tree as the table in the MD's room. Around this massive table, several chairs were arranged, and a dozen or so sullen faces were seated on them, staring back at Rhea, none of whom acknowledged her. There was no music to lighten the mood in the boardroom.

Dr. Subhash Gupta, the managing director, sat at the head of the table and asked Rhea to sit opposite him so they could face each other. Sitting down, she observed that the table was so large that he seemed far from her. She glanced on either side of her and recognized Dr. Ishwar Nathwani from her department, Dr. Akbar, the senior consultant from oncology, Dr. Harishchandra from paediatrics, and Dr. Vrinda from Gynaecology, the only other woman in the room. The rest were all strangers in suits.

"Good evening, everyone," said Dr Gupta into the mic in front of him on the table. "As you all know, we have convened this emergency board meeting following the developments in the news channels, which have shattered the image of our organization."

He paused and looked around. A couple of members glanced at her as if to let her know she was responsible for everything. The rest of them had their sights firmly on the MD. Dr. Nathwani was staring at the glass of water in front of him.

"I thank all the shareholders for being here at such brief notice," he said, nodding to the people of his right. He was met with nods in return.

"Before we decide on the matter at hand, we would like to allow Dr Rhea Sharma to put forth her side of the story before all of us," said the MD.

Rhea didn't like the sound of it at all. *Her side of the story* meant they already seemed to believe the other side. But she was not a coward and would not be intimidated by all the men in the room. She knew they would expect her to be submissive and timid, something she would never give anyone the satisfaction of seeing from her. She took a deep breath and, with an upright posture, narrated everything that happened on that particular day, how the patient presented, what she did, how she counselled the mother and wife, what Mr Bhaskar, the employer, told her, and every detail of the surgery.

"So you are saying the allegations against you are false?" asked the MD after her narration.

Rhea wanted to remind him that they had levelled the allegations both against her and the hospital, but she thought better of it.

"Absolutely, sir," replied Rhea confidently.

She didn't know if it was her imagination, but she felt she heard Dr Nathwani snicker from his place. There were a few minutes of silence as everyone digested everything she had said.

"As a senior consultant and being from the same

department, what is your opinion about the matter, Dr Nathwani?" asked the MD.

Now, all eyes were on Dr Nathwani as if he were the judge and the jury. Rhea didn't want to look at him and kept her gaze focused on the MD. Dr Nathwani shifted his massive frame in his chair and leaned on the table to speak into the mic. It was no secret that he enjoyed being the centre of attention.

"I have no idea who is right or wrong here, and that is a question that only Dr Rhea can answer. We have to believe what she says," he said without looking at her.

Rhea didn't know if she was being sarcastic or genuine.

"But we must consider that irrespective of whether she is right or wrong, the media is putting forth solid proof of wrongdoing here. It doesn't help that there are people within our organization who have corroborated their allegations. This entire media coverage is ruining our reputation, and we need to do something about it as soon as possible," he said, looking at the board members, who nodded in approval.

The MD nodded in approval as well, and Rhea knew this would not bode well for her.

"That is what we were thinking when we discussed the same with our lawyers," said the MD, pointing to the men on his left, whom, until then, Rhea was not aware as being lawyers.

"So let me be frank with you, Dr. Rhea," said the MD, looking at her. We have conducted an internal investigation and have found that the news channels are correct. Even the Emergency Medicine specialist has confirmed the same on condition of anonymity, and we will not reveal his data to the media."

Rhea was unsurprised by the revelation. She would

have guessed that the emergency medicine specialist did it to gain some brownie points with the management. What better way to improve your prospects than to provide evidence against someone else while remaining anonymous when things go wrong?

"So, as Dr Nathwani said, this media coverage reflects badly on us, something we cannot afford to do in this competitive business. We employ hundreds of staff from doctors to housekeeping, and their livelihood depends on us, so we cannot let them down if something happens to our organization," preached the MD.

Rhea knew he didn't care about the employees. People were fired, and new ones were appointed in their places in the blink of an eye. All that the MD or the board cared about was profits, whether by *fair means or foul*.

"So we have decided to release a statement to the press that we are letting you go from our organization. We will compensate the victim's family to distance ourselves from the entire saga. We will not comment on whether you did right or wrong," he said.

Rhea could not believe what she was hearing. *What a ridiculous solution!* What was the point of commenting when his actions were enough for people to know she was wrong? Not only were they firing her, they were also compensating the family. They were saving their skins while throwing her to the wolves. She wanted to remind him that it was he who had pushed her to the brink by hanging the sword of Damocles around her neck, demanding more of her even though she was doing her best. He was the one who had given her an ultimatum, saying that she would be fired if she didn't do better. He was the one who put the idea of doing something *by fair means or foul* into her head. And now, he was firing her when she was in trouble trying to execute what he said. *And if you do get caught, they will throw you under the bus;* Dr Nathwani's were now coming true. If they had already decided what to do with her, why had they called her to the meeting to pretend to hear her side of the story?

"And one more thing. Once we put out our statement to the media, there is a high probability of the medical council terminating your license to practice for a short period as punishment. If it happens, we are ready to rehire you once the termination period is complete, and this entire saga dies in people's minds as a gesture of goodwill since you are our esteemed employee," he said.

With this, they all stood up, leaving Rhea alone in the boardroom, trying to make sense of what had just happened.

Chapter Seven

Rhea spent the next few weeks at home in her pyjamas, lying on the couch, watching the news on TV as the world around her fell apart. Within a week of being fired from her job, the medical council revoked her license to practice for a year, just as the MD had predicted. This meant that she couldn't practice medicine in any hospital across the country for the next 12 months. The local news channels made a big deal about the surgery she had performed, criticizing her morals and even questioning her educational qualifications. Reporters and protestors camped outside her apartment building, making it difficult for security personnel to keep them out. Her phone kept ringing with calls from relatives, friends, and reporters asking for a statement or giving unsolicited advice. After a while, she turned off her phone to avoid the constant interruptions.

Rhea stayed in her apartment unmoved and unnerved, as if nothing unusual had happened. At first, after the board meeting, when she was fired from her job, she was seething at the board members of White Arc. She had toiled hard for three years at the hospital and was happy with her work, the recognition she received, and her paycheque. But then, Dr Gupta pushed her to the limits, demanding that she increase her volume of cases by any means possible and by Dr

Nathwani, who used devious means to poach her patients. When she had done as they expected her, nobody there had come to her aid, and in fact, they blamed her to safeguard their interests and the hospital's reputation. And it had worked like a charm because after she had been dismissed, everyone seemed to have forgotten the hospital and trained their guns only on her.

Then, she directed her anger towards the patient and the family. The mother and wife had begged her to do anything possible for the patient, and the employer had declared that cost was not a factor. She realized that after the news of the death of the worker broke, his employees turned against him, and he had gone to the media and reported what had happened to the patient to deflect the attention away from him, just like what the hospital had done. Of course, the patient's family never blamed her even once, even though they had been pressurized several times live on TV, but that didn't provide any solace to Rhea.

Finally, she directed her anger toward the reporters and the media, targeting her for their TRPs' sake. There were so many problems in the country: so many scams by politicians, so many corrupt police officers torturing innocent citizens every day, and so many issues plaguing the women in the country. Still, they seemed obsessed with the one case she had operated on. So much had been spoken about her, and her reputation had been tarnished. She vowed to avenge the wrong that had been done to her one day.

Despite whatever happened, Rhea didn't shed a tear, as she was much stronger than letting her emotions get the best of her. She refused to feel sorry for herself and kept her head high. Even though her mind was in turmoil regarding her future, she persevered after the initial days of anger. For a month following the incident, she never left the confines of her apartment, and as the days went by, the crowd outside her apartment building dwindled. Eventually, people forgot about her and moved on with their lives. Unfortunately, the damage to Rhea's reputation was irreversible.

"Why don't you go out for a walk?" her father's voice broke her train of thought.

She hadn't realized he had entered the living room and occupied his usual place on the armchair, dressed in his white Kurta pyjama. When she looked at him, she realized, for the first time in a long while, how much he had aged. While she had spent years studying and obsessing about her work, she had not paid attention to the deepening wrinkles on his face or how he winced when he sat down because his knees hurt. But one thing that had not changed about him was the love in his eyes for her.

Ever since childhood, he had always been her closest confidante and best friend, with whom she shared every detail of her life. She never needed to have any other best friend because of him. However, as the years passed, she shared less and less of her personal life with him but still approached him for advice, and he was always there for her. "I don't feel like it right now, Dad," Rhea said, feeling safe in the apartment.

"It will do you a world of good. How long will you stay within these walls?" he asked.

"For a year at least. It's not like I will be working any time soon," she said, still lying on the sofa and staring vacantly.

Her father remained silent because he knew she was right. Rhea had never considered anything in life besides surgery, so it was hard for her to fathom what she would do in the coming year. He continued sipping his coffee, which he had brought along, while she stared at the ceiling.

"Do you believe all those news channels and reports that I did something wrong?" she asked, sitting up to face him after a while.

It was something she had wanted to ask him ever since the news broke. She had never discussed what exactly had happened with him except for telling him that she had done no wrong. Her father looked at her kindly like he always did.

"As a father, whether you are right or wrong, you are always my daughter, and I will always love you," he said, placing his coffee cup on the table.

It had been long since her father told her he loved her because they hardly spoke their hearts out when Rhea was studying and working. She was never even home to have a heart-to-heart conversation most of the time. So it felt great to hear him say it.

"But you are mature enough to know whether you are right or wrong. So you tell me, what do you feel?" he asked, seeing her eye to eye.

She knew her father too well. He would never cast aspersions on her. Instead, he would eke out the answers from her, just like he always did. *Self-realization* was what he used to call it back when she was a kid.

"I don't think I did anything wrong," replied Rhea, repeating the same sentence she had been saying to everyone for the past few months.

"If you didn't, I don't think you would have asked for my opinion," he said with a smile.

Rhea moved her gaze away from him immediately. She knew he had caught her off guard with his response. She had convinced herself that she had done no wrong.

"I just did what needs to be done to stay ahead. I did

nothing that someone else in my place would not have done," she said, looking at the balcony and the blue sky beyond.

Her father inhaled deeply and nodded like he understood what she said. After all, he had seen more life than her, even though he was not from the medical profession.

"To succeed, you don't have to follow the crowd. Create your own path and never harm others to stay ahead," he replied.

"You do not understand what a cutthroat business the medical profession has become, Dad," replied Rhea "It's not like your days when the family doctor used to visit your home with a briefcase."

"You are right; I do not understand your profession," he said. "But any profession that makes you do more harm than good, especially if it is medicine, then there is something seriously wrong about it. And it is certainly not how we have raised you to be," he said.

He does believe I am wrong, she thought to herself, and that thought stung more than all the accusations of TV channels and the hospital board.

"It's a man's world, Dad," said Rhea, shaking her head. "If a man breaks the rules, he is forgiven, but if a woman does the same, she is crucified. I want to prove to everyone that a woman is no less than a man."

"If you want to break the rules, break them, but see that something good comes out of it," he said kindly. "And if you think that men are wrong and want to prove that women are better, then do it the right way, not using the same path taken by men, which you consider wrong in the first place."

"But if you don't do what others do, you will lose your opportunity and be left behind," said Rhea, remembering what Dr Nathwani had told her.

"The beauty of life is that it keeps giving you opportunities to climb back up every time you fall. It just depends on you as to what you want to make of those opportunities," her father said.

Both of them sat in silence, with Rhea contemplating his words. He had said so much without saying a single word about the incident in the hospital. It was a gift he possessed.

"So now I don't have a job, can't work for a year, and people think I am a crook. What am I supposed to do now, Dad?" she asked.

"Get married!" her mother said, bustling into the room out of nowhere, as usual. "This is the best time to get married."

Rhea always marvelled at how her mother listened to every word, even when she wasn't present in the room, and how she brought the topic of her marriage into every discussion.

"Absolutely not!" thundered Rhea.

"And why not?" asked her mother, sitting beside her on the sofa's edge.

"Because I am not in the right state of mind to get married," said Rhea. "Besides, on what basis am I going to look for a husband when I don't have a job or reputation when I am most vulnerable?"

"Who asked you to hunt for a groom? Am I dead?" asked her mother. "And why can't you get married now? Is the boy marrying you or your job? Don't homemakers get married?"

Rhea looked away from her mother in disgust. They were opposites and never seemed to agree on anything, especially marriage. Rhea found it impossible to confer to her conservative and old-fashioned opinions.

"Why don't you go on a vacation?" her father asked,

breaking in. "I don't remember the last time you went on a holiday!"

"Are you out of your mind?" asked her mother, turning her attention and wrath to Rhea's father. "She is 33 years old, unmarried, without a job, with people speaking ill of her everywhere, and you are asking her to go on a holiday?"

"Why not?" asked her father, ignoring her mother and looking at Rhea. "I think it'll freshen up your mind, and you can come back energized with a fresh perspective on life."

Rhea found the idea appealing. She was still struggling to walk down the city streets after a recent incident, so the thought of going to a place where she was unknown and could explore was inviting. She had no other commitments and had spent the last 15 years studying and the previous three years working without a break. Her dedication had allowed her to save enough money to cover the year she planned to take off. She needed a break, not just physically but mentally as well.

"Where do you suggest I go?" she asked, her father warming up to the idea.

"Leh Ladakh?" he reminded her with a wink.

Rhea remembered the conversation at the dinner table a month ago. Her brother Rahul had paid for a Leh Ladakh trip before he was supposed to join work at his company. But they had asked him to report early, so he could neither go on the trip nor get a refund. She hoped he hadn't given away the tickets to someone else.

"It can be my first solo trip!" she said enthusiastically.

"Are you both out of your mind?" glowered her mother, standing up and placing her hands on her head dramatically, which made her look like a laughing Buddha to Rhea. "You want to go on a trip now, that too all alone. Are you forgetting that you are a girl?"

"Why not?" asked her father, still looking at Rhea. "Your mother just said that you are 33 years old. If you are old enough to marry, you are surely old enough to go on a solo trip. After all, marriage is scarier than a Leh Ladakh trip,"

Both Rhea and her father laughed as her mother stomped out of the room angrily.

Chapter Eight

Rhea gazed out of the airplane window and was awestruck by the majestic sight that greeted her. Although not easily impressed, the snow-covered mountain peaks of the Himalayas left her mesmerized. The airplane was flying low, preparing for the descent, and the clouds seemed to hug it, making it difficult to distinguish where the white mountains ended and the sky began. Everything blended like one white canvas sheet. From her vantage point, it was hard to believe that the Himalayas housed some of the tallest mountains in the world. Moreover, it was even harder to comprehend that six countries shared these mountains as their borders.

As the pilot's voice crackled through the intercom, announcing the imminent landing, she shifted her gaze from the icicles outside to the plane's interior. She fastened her seatbelt and relaxed her head against the headrest, her eyes closed. It was surreal that she had made the trip. At first, she only agreed to her father's suggestion to irritate her mother and get her off her back. But as she thought more, she realized that a trip would do her a world of good, and the timing couldn't have been better. This was probably the first and last time she would ever travel alone, and it was a way for her to escape the hustle and bustle of city life. Besides, she had nothing to lose since, for the first time, she had all the free time in the world.

The slow descent of the plane moved her gaze back to

the window as the mountain tops got closer and more prominent every second. She tried to look for the landing strip but found it hard to spot amidst the dense fog and the dazzling white of the snow-capped mountains. *What would happen if the plane struck one mountain? Was it a certain death?* If it were, it would be over in the blink of an eye. She chuckled, thinking it would be a shame since she would reach heaven without exploring this heavenly place.

Finally, she caught sight of the narrow landing strip below, like a black line drawn across a white sheet of paper. As the line got closer, it widened into a path, and when the airplane's tires thudded against the tarmac, she realized that she had made it. She was in Ladakh, *the land of the high passes* amidst the Himalayas, *the abode of snow*.

As Rhea stood at the plane's door, waiting to descend the airplane stairs, she noticed that the air felt lighter and breathing was challenging. This was not surprising since they were at a high altitude. Just as she was focussing on her breathing, a sudden roar startled her, and she had to cover her ears to protect herself from the deafening noise. Looking up, she saw a fighter jet soaring above them.

"There is an air base right next to us," said the smiling flight attendant at the door, seeing Rhea's baffled expression.

Rhea nodded as she kept her eyes on the fighter jet. It was speeding away into the distance until it was merely a speck, making her realize the harsh reality of war. She had read about wars in the newspapers, watched fighter jets circling the air on television, and always thought of it happening somewhere far away at the border in a different world. However, now she found herself at that border, amid it all, giving her goosebumps.

They had to walk from the airplane to the airport since

the Ladakh airport did not have a shuttle service or an aero bridge. Although it was a short walk, the cold weather and high altitude made breathing difficult and caused a chill to run down her spine. To make matters worse, she was dressed lightly for the hot weather in Mumbai, wearing black jeans and a red peasant top. She couldn't wait to get to the hotel and change into something warmer.

After collecting her luggage from the airport's carousel, she quickly got into a taxi without any trouble. Unlike Mumbai airport, the crowd was sparse, and she was pleased when the driver informed her that they had reached their destination within just 10 minutes in Leh. As she got out of the taxi, she looked at her hotel building, which had an ancient charm, unlike the modern high rises in Mumbai that she was accustomed to. The three-storey building was made of colourful brick and mortar and looked like it had been standing there for a hundred years. When she entered the small reception area, an ancient Tibetan man, who was shorter than her, welcomed her warmly and escorted her to her room on the top floor. Rhea gave him a tip for his effort, which he accepted with a toothless grin.

The room was relatively small, even smaller than her bedroom in Mumbai. It had a wooden bed, a fireplace, a bathroom with a mirror, and a small wooden cupboard for her clothes. It looked like a bachelor pad, which Rahul would have been content with the bare necessities. Rhea didn't complain since the room was clean. She freshened up and changed into warm clothes. By the time she was done, it was already dark outside. She looked out the window and saw the colourful vibrance of the city. The old man brought her some piping hot Kahwa tea while he lit the fireplace. A cool breeze seeped in as she stood by the window sipping her tea, making her feel warm and cozy. She didn't want to leave the comfort of her room, but the more she looked outside, the more inviting the sight became. After a while, she couldn't resist the temptation and decided to explore Leh's nightlife. She walked down the stairs and headed out into the city.

As Rhea walked out of the hotel, she was hit by the cold weather, as if a truck had struck her, despite her wearing multiple layers of warm clothes. She wore dark blue denim, a black turtleneck top, a red sweater, and a red hoodie with black boots. However, the layers of clothing didn't provide enough protection against the cold. The cobble-stoned streets were illuminated by street lights that cast an orange hue, reminding Rhea of White Arc Hospital's sixth floor. She immediately scolded her for thinking about the hospital. She turned her attention to the shops lining both sides of the street. They seemed to sell various items, from lamps to counterfeit branded watches. Tourists walked carefree while shop owners tried to lure them into their stores. She followed the colourful buntings on the street lamps and found herself in several Pashmina stalls. She bought a few shawls for her mother and then visited shops that sold souvenirs, postcards, local artwork, and handicrafts. Before she knew it, she was carrying two large shopping bags in each hand.

By then, she was both hungry and tired and looked around for a place to eat. Her eyes fell on an open-air eatery with an old, rusted, tilted board hung outside that said *Shainaz's Kitchen*, and she walked into it. It was a tiny outlet with bamboo chairs and tables placed close to each other, so people had to squeeze about to get around the place. The air was thick with the sweet aroma of kebabs, and people seemed to be devouring them with gusto. There were around ten small tables, all occupied, and Rhea stood there with her shopping bags, looking for a place to sit.

"Come with me, *didi*; I will get you a place to sit," said a polite voice behind her.

When Rhea turned around, she was a slender, beautiful girl in a pink hijab smiling at her. Rhea followed the girl to the corner, where she hurriedly pulled out a small folding steel table and an empty chair from an adjacent table.

"Thank you very much," said Rhea settling in. "Are you Shainaz?"

"Oh no, *didi*. That's my mother," said the girl with a shy smile, holding the edge of the hijab to her face. "My name is Sania."

Sania seemed to be in her late teens, and Rhea guessed her height to be around 5 feet 4 inches since she was a couple of inches shorter than Rhea. She was blessed with a beautiful round face with milky white skin. *All my aunts would have been so happy seeing the colour of her skin,* thought Rhea. Growing up, she always heard her relatives say, *You are so beautiful if only you were fairer.* It always irritated Rhea when she was younger since she found nothing wrong with her dusky complexion, but it no longer mattered as she got older. She had enough boys swooning over her in college to know that her aunts were wrong.

"So, what is the specialty in your mother's kitchen?" asked Rhea.

"I think you will enjoy the kebabs and the biryani," she said with a twinkle in her eye.

Rhea asked for a plate of both. Sania hurried to the opposite end and entered the door, which Rhea assumed to be the kitchen. She returned within no time and stood next to her. A young woman traveling all by herself seemed to intrigue Sania. She asked Rhea who she was and what she did for a living.

"You are a surgeon?" said Sania, her mouth agape.

Rhea smiled.

"And you are so beautiful, too!" said Sania.

Rhea blushed with a hint of embarrassment.

"And you have come all the way from Mumbai alone?" continued Sania, wide-eyed.

"Yes. It's no big deal," Rhea said, amused by the girl's curiosity.

"It is a big deal, *didi*," replied Sania, leaning forward and whispering, "Here, girls don't even leave their houses alone."

What a sad life it must be. To be bound by rules, not be able to do what you want, and to fear men who made those rules in the first place. She imagined Sania's mother forcing her to get married soon, just like her mother would have done many years ago. *At least Sania's mother would not differ from her mother in that respect,* thought Rhea mournfully.

Someone called out from inside the kitchen, and Sania ran over. She returned with Rhea's hot meal and proceeded to the counter where some customers were waiting to pay their bills. Rhea tasted the food, praying it would be half decent as she expected it to be, but to her surprise, it was delicious.

"Do you like the food, *didi*?" asked Sania, hurrying back to Rhea's makeshift table.

"It's one of the best I have ever had," replied Rhea. "Your mother is a real magician."

Sania twirled around in delight as if Rhea had complimented her cooking, and Rhea couldn't help but laugh.

"Wait *didi*," said Sania, "I'll get my mother. She will be happy to hear it from you."

Sania hurried away, and her earnestness amused Rhea,

so she didn't want to disappoint her. It was like a whole different world where a compliment was enough to cheer someone up, unlike the cutthroat world she had come from. Sania returned with a middle-aged woman who looked so strikingly similar to Sania that they seemed like the present and future versions of each other to Rhea.

"*Didi*, this is my mother. She is the *Shainaz* in the kitchen," she said amidst childlike giggles.

"It's very nice to meet you. Not only is your food one of the best I have tasted, but your daughter is one of the most delightful people I have ever met," said Rhea, smiling with her hands folded in a respectful namaste.

"You are very kind," said Shainaz with folded hands.

Sania brought another chair, and they all sat down together, engrossed in their conversation as if the rest of the world didn't exist. Sania introduced Rhea to her mother as if they had been friends for a long time. Sania explained that Rhea was a surgeon who had travelled alone to Leh. Rhea then shared her plans for the two weeks she was staying in Leh. Shainaz was impressed and looked at Rhea with admiration. The fact that Rhea was a doctor who performed surgeries seemed to elevate her status even more in their eyes.

"We need more women like you in our country. Only then will women have a foothold in this male-dominated society," said Shainaz.

Rhea was taken aback by her statement since she didn't expect Shainaz to be such a progressive thinker. Even her mother would never have said such a thing.

"Along with all the other things that you have planned for the trip, one thing you must do is go on the Chadar Trek along the Zanskar River," said Shainaz.

"Absolutely *didi*," added Sania.

"Is it? I am not much of a trekker and have contacted no one for it," said Rhea.

"Then you are in luck, *didi*. My brother runs an agency that organizes the Chadar Trek, and we are shamelessly promoting it to you," Sania said with her trademark giggle.

Rhea was unsure if she wanted to go on the trek since she was not used to such strenuous physical activity. Her body was more attuned to standing in one place and operating for hours together rather than walking miles on a treacherous plane. But she didn't want to refuse both of them outright.

"Don't worry, my son is a decent boy," said Shainaz, looking at the uncertainty on Rhea's face.

"Oh no! That's not what I meant," said Rhea, embarrassed that she had given the wrong impression. "It's just that I don't know if the trek will be too much for me."

"You have travelled all the way from Mumbai alone. You operate on people. So trust me, this trek will be a piece of cake for you," said Sania.

Rhea couldn't help but laugh at her enthusiasm. She agreed, took his address from them, and planned to visit the place the next day.

Chapter Nine

"Can I meet Saahil?" Rhea asked as she placed her backpack on the counter.

The trek was yet to begin, but Rhea was already exhausted from carrying her black backpack to the trekking agency that Sania had recommended the previous night. In addition to that, she was wearing multiple layers of clothing, including a thick red sweater, a black windcheater, black woollen trousers, black boots, and a black balaclava on her head. After dinner, Sania convinced Rhea to go on the Zanskar trek and suggested all the necessary items, including a torch, batteries, gum boots, a trekking pole, extra sunscreen, socks, etc. Sania's enthusiasm was contagious, and she had even accompanied Rhea for another round of late-night shopping. During their shopping spree, Sania shared detailed information about the Zanskar and Indus rivers and how they merged at the Sangam confluence. Rhea felt like she was packing for a trip within a trip, but Sania's excitement made her look forward to the adventure.

"They become one, but they are still not one," she said mysteriously.

Like my mother and me, chuckled Rhea. It was supposed to be a three-day trek. The Zanskar River was used for rafting during the summer, but now, during winter, when it froze, it formed a sheet and hence was called *the chadar* or a bed sheet. Sania said it would be one of the most beautiful sights Rhea had ever witnessed.

"Who's asking?" a voice cut her chain of thought.

Rhea glanced across the counter and saw a young man who appeared to be in his late twenties. He had a chiselled square jaw, fair skin with stubble, and brown eyes that resembled hers. His long, wavy hair fell across his forehead. As he stood up and walked towards the counter, Rhea, though not someone to be easily impressed by good looks, was momentarily taken aback by his striking features.

"I am Rhea Sharma from Mumbai," said Rhea, recovering quickly in a business-like tone. "Shainaz directed me to this agency and asked me to speak to her son Saahil."

She saw him size her up but did it casually as if she were just another customer.

"He's on leave today. Fill this," he said brusquely, thrusting a register towards her and returning to sit behind the counter.

Rhea grabbed the register, wondering what his problem was since he seemed as cold as the weather in Leh. She stood at the counter and filled all the necessary information into the register, like her contact details, the emergency number of her father in case something happened to her, and also a consent form stating that nobody could hold the agency responsible if she were to die during the trek, *just like a patient taken up for surgery*. Once she was done, she quietly pushed the register back to him, and he scrutinized the same.

"Are you sure you want to go on the trek?" he asked her impatiently without getting up from his chair.

"I wouldn't be here if I wasn't sure, would I?" she replied.

She could see he wasn't satisfied with her response,

but she didn't care. Nobody could belittle her, especially a man. She had lived in a man's world all her life, fighting and winning against them; a lowly trek operator would not change that.

"Manish, get madam's medical done," he called out to a porter without looking at Rhea.

The cheerful Nepali porter stood out in stark contrast to the gloomy guy at the counter. He guided Rhea to a nearby room that was bustling with activity. Inside were about 15 people, all with large backpacks and dressed similarly to her, standing in an unorganized line. They were waiting to have their temperatures, weight, and oxygen saturation levels checked in a brightly lit room.

"Oye madamji, please go ahead, ladies first," said a middle-aged *Sardarji* in a bright pink turban, red fleece jacket, and green heavy woollen trousers.

Rhea had to hold back her laughter, looking at his ensemble.

"No, thank you," she replied, standing at the back. "First come, first serve."

"That is what I say when I visit the bar," he said, bowing dramatically in deep respect.

Everyone around giggled. Instantly, it seemed to break the ice in the room, and Rhea felt more comfortable.

"Hi, I am Divya, and this is my husband, Prashanth," said the lady in front of her.

She was the same height as Rhea and had the same complexion, with a tiny mole on the left side of her chin. Unlike Rhea's flowing hair, she had curly locks that came up to her shoulders. Her husband waved at her cheerfully.

"Nice to meet you," replied Rhea and introduced herself.

"Thank God you are here. I was afraid of being the only woman on the trek," said Divya, hugging her trekking pole.

Rhea didn't understand this perennial need for a woman to have another woman for the company since she was raised to be bold and independent by her father despite the conservative views of her mother.

"We are on our honeymoon," she added.

Rhea looked at her, surprised but impressed. You rarely hear of someone honeymooning in Leh Ladakh. *But this is how it should be,* she thought. Do what you feel, not what you are expected to do. At least it made up for her earlier comment that had irritated Rhea.

While she waited in the queue, she also got to know a few other trekkers in the group. The loud, hefty *Sardarji* was Surjith Singh, a contractor back in Punjab who dealt with laying water pipelines. His business partner Anil Sharma, a short, stout middle-aged man from whom he bought the pipes, accompanied him. They seemed like an odd pair at the trek not only because of *Sardarji's* colourful dressing sense compared to Sharmaji's understated presence but also because *Sardarji* was loud and Sharmaji was quiet. There was also a group of 5 college boys, high on testosterone, who made a lot of noise, and she knew that each of them was vying for her attention despite being over ten years younger than her.

After finishing their medical check-ups and passing them all, the group was transported by tempo traveller to *Shingra Yokma,* the starting point of the trek, half an hour from the office. As soon as they arrived and exited the vehicle, she noticed two things: the biting cold weather and many other tempo travellers in the area, all carrying trekkers from different agencies.

Their group huddled around the arrogant counter guy whose name no one knew but who was now referred to as the *Team Leader*. In a dull, monotonous voice, he instructed them to walk slowly in a single file, drink plenty of fluids, and not do anything stupid, as if he loathed each of them.

"Where do we pee?" asked Divya, looking around the mountainside.

"Over there," he said, pointing to a tent at the far end of the mountainside. "There will be similar facilities along the way."

Rhea saw the colour drain from Divya's face when she saw the run-down nature of the *facility*.

"Oye, better to do your business into the river than risk going there," said *Sardarji,* which no one found funny except for the college boys who began howling.

"If anyone has second thoughts about the trip, they can decide right now since the tempo traveller will return to the office," said the team leader, looking specifically at Rhea, which annoyed her.

Everyone except Rhea laughed because they thought he was kidding. They both exchanged icy stares and began their trek.

Only when they began walking did Rhea notice the sheer magnificence of the surroundings. The Zanskar river flowed lazily with its peripheries on either side, completely frozen. They hiked in a single file, with the team leader leading and Manish and two other porters at the back hauling huge bags. The gigantic mountains on either side were draped in white, glistening in the little available sunlight, faintly visible in the dense fog. Rhea had to draw herself away from the landscape and focus on the slippery path to avoid falling.

The first two hours were filled with nonstop chatter

from the college boys, and *Sardarji's* comments enthralled the group. But after that, they became weary and grew silent, concentrating on their steps and every breath they inhaled.

"I think we need to take a break. I am feeling cold," said Divya, who was walking in front of Rhea.

"No!" shouted the team leader from ahead. "The colder you feel, the faster you walk. That's the only way to beat the cold. And keep hydrating."

Rhea involuntarily took a few sips of water from her bottle. She was tired, but she was holding on. She didn't want to be the one asking for a break and holding up the group. Moreover, she didn't want to give the team leader the satisfaction of thinking she was weak. She slipped more than a couple of times, on the verge of falling onto the ice, but held on somehow.

They finally broke for lunch and settled in one of the makeshift campsites where the relief on everyone's faces was evident. Rhea removed her soaking wet socks and boots and left them out to dry while her bare feet touched the cold, hard ground. The porters unwrapped their wares, and soon, the smell of food wafted into everyone's nostrils.

"I didn't think it would be this hard," said Divya to Rhea.

Nor did Rhea. She was panting with exertion, and her pulse was bounding, but she was happy that she had made it this far. They had completed just a few hours of the trek, but for her, it was like crossing a huge hurdle she was proud of.

"Oye, no way, boy. Don't do it," she heard the *Sardarji* say.

They all turned towards the group and saw that Avakash, one of the college boys, had stripped to his boxers, showing off his chiselled body and washboard abs. He posed for everyone with his eyes firmly on Rhea, who looked the other way in disgust. And then, to everyone's disbelief, he jumped into the ice-cold water, swam around for a couple of minutes, and then jumped out as if it was no big deal. All the boys in the group applauded his bravery and began coaxing *Sardarji* to jump into the water, who refused vehemently, saying that he didn't want to die a virgin.

"What stupidity," Divya said to Rhea, who didn't acknowledge her because she didn't care and because her eyes were on the team leader.

He completely ignored their group and watched an old porter of a different team haul a heavy backpack on his shoulders. Rhea was amazed to see how detached he was from the team he was leading. Lunch was a brief affair, and they were soon off on the gruelling trek again.

The rest of the day went by without incident, and the only thing they all had in common was exhaustion. The only person who kept his spirits high and spoke nonstop was the Sardarji, and Rhea was impressed by his stamina and vitality.

As the sun set and cast long shadows, a hundred campfires illuminated the mountainside. After a tiring six-hour trek, the group decided to stop for the night. Rhea, who wasn't accustomed to such strenuous physical activity, found the trek particularly challenging. The tents were set up quickly, and the porters lit the fires. The group began playing a friendly game of snowball fight, which quickly turned into a fun war. Rhea, who initially refused to be drawn into it, soon got in when Avakash repeatedly bombarded her with snowballs, and her competitive spirit overcame her maturity. Soon, she was giggling and flinging snowballs, especially enjoying *Sardarji's* reaction, jumping around and screaming like a child whenever the cold snowball hit him. She was back to being the little girl who loved to play such games with her friends.

She saw Pradyumna, the tall, lanky, bearded college boy, approach her with a snowball in hand from the corner of her eye. She knew what he was planning, but she turned around and flung a snowball at him with her catlike reflexes. She caught him unaware, but her aim was not as good as her reflex, and unfortunately, she hit the team leader who was walking a little distance away, minding his own business, staying away from all the childishness. The snowball struck him flush on his face, and Rhea was just about to laugh when, to her horror, she saw blood streak from the corner of his face.

Everyone rushed towards him, and Rhea noticed that there was a small gash just above his right eyebrow, which was oozing blood.

"A shard of ice must have grazed his skin," said *Sardarji* worriedly.

"I am really sorry. Let me have a look; I am a doctor," she said earnestly.

But he looked at her in disgust and walked away, leaving her both sorry and angry at his behaviour. The incident dampened everyone's mood; they were too tired anyway from the trek. Hence, they had dinner and slept in their respective tents.

#

Rhea woke up early the next morning feeling stiff as a mummy. Every muscle in her body ached from the trek the previous day, and her bones felt like they would snap like twigs due to the cold. Even slipping out of her sleeping bag was difficult.

"I need a pee partner," said Divya, peeping into the tent.

Why did she want Rhea to accompany her when she

81

had a husband available? She didn't voice her opinion but walked along with her laboriously since she had to go anyway.

"I feel like an ice stupa, cold and ready to shed water," said Divya, giggling and shivering simultaneously. She clutched the shawl she had worn over her warm clothing.

That was more information than what Rhea needed to know.

"It's an invention by somebody from Leh, by the way," said Divya, volunteering information Rhea was not interested in. "I mean the Ice Stupa. In winter, they freeze water into a mini mountain and use it in summer for their fields."

Good for them, thought Rhea dryly. Luckily, she didn't have to build an ice stupa since she was from Mumbai.

They all assembled with their backpacks and trekking poles for breakfast, and to Rhea's relief, all of them seemed to struggle as much as her that morning. The team leader had a white plaster on the side of his face, and she felt guilty about it. She considered apologizing to him again but decided against it since he refused to meet her gaze.

On the second day of their trek, the team found it slightly easier to navigate through the surroundings despite their tired and aching bodies. They played Antakshari while walking in a straight line like penguins in Antarctica. Rhea didn't know a single song, so she admired the surroundings instead. They walked on the frozen periphery of the river while the centre flowed lazily. The fog was as thick as cotton, making it difficult to see anything beyond an arm's length. The singing stopped when they had to crawl through a tiny passage between the flowing river and the mountain, which lasted almost an hour. By the end, Rhea's hands and knees felt like they would drop off because of frostbite. It was also the first time the team leader checked on each of them, including Rhea. Since they were too tired to go on, the team leader ended the trek early that day.

After the tents were put up and the fires were lit, everyone gathered around the warmth of the campfire under the twinkling stars. *Sardarji* shared his unsuccessful attempts to find the right woman and his decision to remain a bachelor. The college boys advised him how to impress women, but he shrugged it off, believing it was too late. Afterward, the attention shifted to Divya and Prashanth as they shared their love story. They revealed that they fell in love while studying to become architects, got married despite their parents' objections, and were now on their honeymoon.

"No wonder we heard some noises in your tent last night," teased Avakash.

"I wish," Prashanth replied, laughing. "I was hard, but that was because my body was frozen."

Rhea couldn't help but laugh, seeing Divya's face turn beet red with embarrassment while the boys hooted and teased Prashanth, and he gamely fended them off. When they asked her about what she did for a living, she explained the field of surgery to them. Divya asked a lot of questions and was impressed. *Sardarji* wanted to know if surgery was available to help him lose weight. Rhea said there were but advised him to do two more Zanskar treks instead. She was careful not to mention which hospital she used to work in since she didn't want them to know about what had happened to her. She was having a great time under the stars in the biting cold in an alien land with strangers friendlier than her colleagues with whom she had worked for years.

Rhea wrapped herself in warm clothes and snuggled into her sleeping bag that night. She tried her best to fall asleep, but despite her fatigue, she couldn't do so. She slipped in and out of a dream and woke up every time. She dreamt of herself being admitted to a hospital, even though she was perfectly fine. The doctor was a young kid, the same one whom she had operated for appendicitis. He seemed to have a wicked smile when he saw her. He looked up at her and informed her she had appendicitis and needed to be operated on immediately. She kept yelling that she was fine, but no one was listening to her. The next moment, she was strapped onto the operating table, and the boy was operating on her.

"She is dead. Shift her to the morgue," he declared.

"No, I am not!" screamed Rhea, but again, no one listened to her.

A cloth was placed on her face, and she was wheeled somewhere. She was shifted into an ice-cold freezer, and the door was shut. Rhea screamed, but no voice came out of her throat.

She woke up gasping in the frosty night air. She looked around the tent, and it took a moment for her to convince herself that it was not the freezer in the morgue but her tent in the middle of nowhere. She struggled to unzip the sleeping bag and gulped in the water from her thermos, which made her feel worse since it was freezing cold. It had been a long time since she had had a nightmare. She got into her sleeping bag and tried to fall back to sleep.

#

The following day, during breakfast, Rhea felt awful because she had been unable to sleep. When she placed her hand on her forehead, she realized she had a fever and couldn't eat her breakfast because she was afraid she would vomit. However, she didn't want to tell anyone because she didn't want to worry them. Additionally, she didn't want the team leader to think she was weak, as he had expected her to be.

It was the third day, and it was time to return to base camp. The boys seemed to be at their goofy best. One bent down and gulped in a palmful of the icy river water.

"Oye, I just pooped into it this morning," declared *Sardarji.*

Everyone burst out laughing, but that made Rhea only more sick. She noticed that the team leader looked back in disgust at *Sardarji.* They trekked the entire day with only a quick lunch break, and with every passing minute, Rhea felt weaker. Soon, it was getting dark.

"Just an hour more, and we will be back at the base camp," declared the team leader from the front.

The entire group breathed a sigh of relief, and the boys gave a cry of victory. It infused fresh energy, and they began walking faster in a single file. Rhea realized she needed to catch up and tried to match their pace. The light had almost faded, and the path was slippery. With her blurring vision and fatigue, she didn't notice a patch of ice that had given way, which others had avoided, and she inadvertently stepped on it, lost her footing, and the last thing she remembered before passing out was the shooting pain in her right arm.

Chapter Ten

Rhea walked carefully from the living room to the front porch, descending three small stairs that spilled onto the busy cobbled street. She held onto the wooden railing for support and sat on the top stair to watch the bustling activity of the street market. The street appeared busier in the morning than when she visited it at night a week ago. In front of her on the footpath, an elderly man had spread out a brown cloth on which he displayed various kinds of nuts, apricot jams, and dried fruits. Rhea observed tourists stopping and bending down to inspect the items. Across the street from her was a jewellery shop, and a large elderly woman wearing a white hijab over her head was setting up the jewellery on a red cloth hung on the wall. Rhea saw a donkey carrying a load of vegetables led by a short Tibetan man. Smoke drifted from the side of the house, where the kitchen had opened early in the morning to cater to customers of *Shainaz's Kitchen*. The mouth-watering aroma of the kebabs filled the air, making it difficult for everyone to resist.

She subconsciously touched the gash on the side of her forehead she had suffered when she had fallen during the Zanskar trek, and though not that bad, it had made her lose consciousness. It required four stitches, which, according to her, was minuscule, but it would leave a scar on her otherwise flawless face. Her left ankle, which had twisted when she had stepped on the loose ice, had suffered a ligament tear, again something which she didn't make a big deal about, though she had to wear an ankle brace and forced her to hobble around. Her only regret was that when she had fallen to the ground, she had held out her right hand to break the fall, which had resulted in a fracture at the wrist when it had come in contact with the ice and was now in a cast.

"*Didi*, why did you walk all the way here by yourself? You could have called me to help you if you needed something," said Sania, hurrying beside her.

"Relax, Sania, I am fine," said Rhea with a smile.

For a change, Sania was not wearing one of her colourful hijabs but a black burkha, just like her mother. It completely covered her except for her round face, which, according to Rhea, was one of the most beautiful she had ever seen. But what Rhea loved more than the fair, slender 18-year-old's beauty was that she was the most cheerful, energetic, and positive person she had ever come across, and she seemed to infuse the same into Rhea every time she spoke to her.

It had been three days since her fall while returning from the Chadar trek. Though she had lost consciousness and couldn't remember the immediate aftermath of it, Sania had updated her on what had happened, how the team leader had carried her in her arms to the nearest medical camp where she received first aid for the wound on her head, her wrist, and ankle. He had then carried her to the base camp where she was bundled into the tempo traveller and shifted to Leh Medical Centre. By then, Rhea had woken up and was in intense pain, but what frightened her most when she opened her eyes was the dilapidated state of the medical centre with its exposed brick walls, creaking beads with torn white sheets, and the untrained personnel. Her first thought was that she would either die at the hands of an incompetent doctor at the hospital or because of an infection later. To add to her horror, she was told that there was only one doctor in the entire hospital at that time who conducted deliveries, sutured wounds, and prescribed fever medications as well.

Luckily, her fracture required only a cast, which the doctor applied under the immense pressure of Rhea's constant orders. When it was done, it wasn't clear who was more relieved, Rhea or the doctor. When she was brought out of the procedure room after the cast application, she was surprised to see Shainaz and Sania there but not as surprised as when she learned that the team leader was Shainaz's son, Saahil. If she had been annoyed by his attitude until then, she was furious now that she knew that he had lied to her. Shainaz insisted that Rhea could not return to her hotel alone since she was still feverish and exhausted despite Rhea's objections, but she had to relent finally.

And it had been three days since she had been living with them, and their hospitality had humbled her. They were not well off or as well off as Rhea assumed someone should be. Their house was a small, one-storied structure next to their eatery, beside the chaotic street market. Sania was always around trying her best to see she didn't have to move a muscle as if Rhea was family and not a tourist she had just bumped into a week ago. Unlike Rhea, she was inquisitive and not ashamed to ask about every detail of her life, including her love life, breakups, etc. Her mother, Shainaz, would see that Rhea was well-fed, and it was hard to refuse the food since it was so good. There was no mention of Sania's father and Rhea, as was her nature did not pry them with questions regarding the same. The only mystery she was concerned about was Saahil's aloofness and attitude towards her. He spoke only to his mother and briefly to Sania but ignored Rhea as if she wasn't there. If there ever was one mystery she wanted to crack, it was him.

"*Didi*, your holiday is getting ruined sitting indoors. Why don't I take you sightseeing?" asked Sania.

Rhea was not the type of person to be intimidated by a fracture, so she was intrigued by the idea. Moreover, she realized she only had one week left of her two-week, life-changing trip to Leh Ladakh and didn't want to spend it indoors. She did not want to return to a future full of uncertainty in Mumbai without enjoying her time here.

"Definitely! What do you suggest?" asked Rhea.

"Why don't we borrow one of Saahil's minivans and visit Shey palace?" asked Sania, excited as if she were doing something illegal.

"As long as you don't get in trouble with that grumpy brother of yours, I don't mind," replied Rhea, rolling her eyes.

"Oh, don't worry, *didi*, I'll manage him," she said.

She stood up and ran over to the payphone on the opposite side of the street, next to the woman selling jewellery. When she returned, she was even more excited.

"It's all set, *didi*. Let's get dressed," she said like a child who is about to get their favourite toy.

They were cruising along the highway within an hour, huddled in the minivan's backseat. Rhea wore blue denim with a black top on which she wore her now permanent red sweater and a black knitted woollen skull cap. Sania had worn a black and grey abaya with a red hijab. After about half an hour, the highway turned into a winding road with acute hairpin curves wound along a mountain. Rhea tried to look atop the hillock the car was winding into and saw a structure of stone that, from afar, looked both magnificent and in ruins. There was a synergy of both old and new within it. The minivan stopped, and the driver looked at Sania for further instructions. She told him to wait for them and that they would not be long. She then helped Rhea climb out of the minivan, and together, they slowly walked along the many stairs that led to the top of the hillock where the Shey palace and monastery were located. Sania held Rhea's hand throughout for support as they explored the different sections of the monastery and the palace. The chief attraction was the 40-foot statue of Buddha, which occupied all three floors of the monastery. Sania guided Rhea through the lower floors, which had a library where ancient manuscripts were preserved, and several beautiful paintings were displayed on the upper floors. Rhea clicked pictures on her cell phone and recorded videos of Sania explaining the different parts of the structure for memories when she returned home. They passed along a wall where the traditional Tibetan cylindrical prayer wheels were attached to a metal spindle. Sania made Rhea rotate each cylinder, telling her it was a Tibetan tradition and would bring her good luck.

After the tour, Rhea's leg hurt, so they descended the stairs, and Sania helped her onto a boulder at the entrance where Rhea could rest.

"What is that building in ruins there?" asked Rhea, pointing at a run-down building she had spotted from the car.

"That is the old Shey Palace, *didi*. The monastery and the new palace were built much later," said Sania.

If only old people like Dr. Nathwani and Dr. Gupta could make way for the younger generation like her in the same way, she thought ruefully. There were a few minutes of silence as Rhea enjoyed the scenery of the city of Ladakh in front of them from the hillock, and Sania went to get them something to nibble on.

"Have you ever been outside Leh Ladakh?" asked Rhea when she returned and handed her a cup of Kahwa tea.

"No, *didi,*" said Sania, cupping the Kahwa tea with both hands.

"Don't you want to leave this place? To see the world? To do something different?" Rhea asked, looking into her eyes.

"There are lots of things I want to do, *didi*. I wanted to become famous for the longest time," she said, laughing. "I didn't know how, but I wanted to. But then I realized I neither have the talent nor the courage to do something that would get me recognized. Besides, for girls like me, the choices are limited. We cannot do what girls in Mumbai or Delhi do," she replied without a hint of remorse.

"I don't agree, Sania," replied Rhea. "Whatever you want in life, you can achieve, no matter where you are. It all depends on how badly you want it."

Sania thought about it for a moment while Rhea continued to scrutinize her. *She is a bright young girl stuck in this tiny pond while there is a sea of opportunity for her outside.* She wondered what she dreamt of, what she wanted in life. *Was she as ambitious as Rhea herself?*

"My mother wouldn't be able to live without me, *didi*. And honestly, I don't think I could live without her," said Sania after a while.

"You can't always think of others, Sania," said Rhea. "You have to think about yourself too. You should be an independent woman."

That was Rhea's mantra in life. She didn't want to be burdened with anything. She lived her life exactly how she wanted to. She had never backed down from a fight in college or at work and was proud of herself. It was one reason she was ready to do anything to succeed, even if it meant treading the narrow path between right and wrong like she had done at White Arc. Sania stared into the distance and nodded as if she understood what Rhea was saying. She remained silent for a while.

"My brother had big dreams, too," she said, looking at Rhea. "I remember when I was eight or nine years old, he was already in college and would tell me he would one day go to a big city, become a software engineer, make loads of money, and move all of us for a better life," she said.

"Then why didn't he do so?" asked Rhea.

Sania remained silent and looked away. Rhea didn't ask anything further, but she assumed that Saahil was one of those individuals who wished for things to happen without putting any effort into it. Many people want everything handed to them on a silver platter, and when it doesn't happen, they blame the world for their failures. That's why Saahil was always in a foul mood and angry with the world.

"*Didi*, what do you think of my brother?" asked Sania out of the blue.

Rhea thought for a while, trying to formulate an answer that would not hurt her feelings.

"You think that he is arrogant and worthless, right?" Sania volunteered herself with a smile.

Sania had perfectly encapsulated Rhea's thoughts about Saahil. There was no way she could think of anything positive in him, despite how he had helped her during her fall at the trek. He had probably done it only because she was his responsibility during the trek. She just smiled, and that was enough to let Sania know that she was right.

"I want to show you something *didi*," she said, leaning towards Rhea, "Will you come with me?"

Rhea was curious about the sudden change in topic but agreed. Sania waved at the minivan driver, who was parked a little distance away, and once he reversed the vehicle towards them, they got in.

"Tashkar," she instructed the driver, who looked back at her curiously but drove away obediently.

Rhea gazed out the car window as it drove through the stunning mountain landscapes, awe-inspiring crevices, and frozen waterfalls down the hill. It felt like a whole new world, something she could never have imagined when she lived in Mumbai. The clouds hung so low she thought she could touch them if she jumped high enough. Sania was unusually quiet and lost in thought as she looked out her window.

After traveling for about half an hour, the car stopped at the banks of a narrow river, which, like the Zanskar, was frozen along the edges on either side but flowing in the middle. They exited the minivan, and Sania helped Rhea hobble on the river bank and settle on a rock.

"Are you okay, *didi*?" asked Sania

"I am fine, Sania," replied Rhea, looking around at the serene surroundings of the river. "What is this place?"

"It's one of the tributaries of the Indus, *didi*," replied Sania with a smile. "This is not the place I wanted to show you. That is on the other side of the river."

Rhea watched as she covered her face with her shawl to act like a niqab, exposing only her eyes. She then waved out to an elderly man who was sitting idly on a small boat on the opposite end of the narrow river. On seeing them, he rowed towards them with surprising agility and helped them climb aboard. He rowed them steadily across the flowing river to the other frozen end. It was a quick ride completed in a few minutes, and once they were ashore, Sania got off the boat and helped Rhea out. Sania dropped some coins into the old man's palms, which he gratefully accepted.

They kept walking quietly as Rhea took in the surroundings. The riverbank they were walking on was surrounded by dense shrubbery, making it seem uninhabited. Tall trees grew so close to each other that it appeared to be a dead end, but it was a delightful picnic spot away from all the noise and pollution, especially for someone from Mumbai. Rhea noticed a clearing amidst the dense foliage, which people seemed to use as a path. As expected, Sania guided her onto that path. They walked for a couple of minutes along it, and Rhea felt like she was walking through a forest with branches shielding any sunlight from penetrating it. Rhea wondered what Sania wanted to show her in the middle of the jungle. Before she could ask Sania, the trees ended abruptly, and they were in an open area with a view that she was not expecting to see.

They were on a tiny hillock, and below them was what seemed to be a village of small houses.

"This is the village of Tashkar, *didi*," Sania said through her niqab, which still covered her face. "It shares its border with India, Pakistan, and China. Do you see that land beyond the fence?"

"Yes," replied Rhea, squinting her eyes and placing her hand above them to shield them from the sunlight. On the mountainside, there was a rudimentary fence made of wood and string.

"That is Pakistan," said Sania.

She had heard and read about the LOC many times, but standing at the border and looking at it felt unreal.

They walked down the hillock, and Rhea needed all of Sania's support to trudge down it since her leg hurt and her arm was in a cast. They entered the village at the foot of the hillock, and Rhea's first impression was that it was all haphazard, with an unpaved road snaking around tiny single-storey brick houses built with no planning, as if a little kid had randomly placed Lego blocks here and there. Rhea saw a naked boy around four years old standing beside an open well, smiling at them. How he ran on the road in such cold weather without clothing was hard for her to understand.

They kept walking along the narrow path, which had never seen a vehicle, looking at the bare brick single-storey cubes of houses side by side.

"There are about 100 families here," Sania said when she saw Rhea scrutinizing the houses. "Their village head governs them. They are poor and live off the farms they cultivate in the back near the foothills. Tourists don't visit this place since there is nothing to see. The locals of Ladakh themselves don't come here because there is nothing for them to do here."

Sania led Rhea to an open area resembling a village meeting place. She explained that this was where the village head addressed the villagers and made decisions regarding their issues. At that moment, Rhea noticed around 15 underdressed or shabbily dressed children of different ages sitting on the cold, bare ground. There was a blackboard with numbers written as if they were learning mathematics. When Rhea saw who the teacher was, she realized why Sania had brought her there.

Chapter Eleven

They looked at each other simultaneously as if it had been choreographed. Dressed in black formal pants, a blue and black chequered sweater, and a black muffler around his neck, Saahil, who until then was animatedly waving his hands and teaching the children with a smile on his face, a smile she had never seen until then, froze. Rhea didn't know what it was about her that annoyed him so much, but in an instant, his smile was replaced by a scowl that was always present when she was around. The children also noticed the change in his demeanour since they all turned around to look at Rhea. She saw his eyes shift from her to Sania and then back to her. He threw the white chalk in his hand in disgust and walked towards them with intent.

"What are you doing here?" he demanded Sania.

"I was just showing Rhea *didi* around," she lied.

Rhea knew that Sania intended for her to see that very scene, Saahil teaching a group of shabbily dressed children in an unknown village, in an attempt to change her opinion about him.

"Of all the places in Leh, you chose this one?" he asked with his hands on his hips, his wavy hair blowing on his face in the wind.

"I j… just…" stammered Sania, holding her niqab

tightly onto her face.

"And since when did you become her tour guide, or are you her maid now?" he asked with repulsion before she could complete her sentence.

"You can't talk to her like that," Rhea interjected angrily, though she knew the comment was directed more at her than Sania.

"You don't need to teach me how to talk to my sister," Saahil replied, looking at her.

Rhea saw the throbbing artery on the side of his forehead.

"Come on, *bhaiyya*," said Sania. "We are just looking around. We are not getting in anyone's way. We'll walk for a bit and leave."

"I have told you many times that this place is not safe, Sania," said Saahil, his voice softening a little.

"But you come here all the time, *bhaiyya*," Sania replied. Why is it safe for you and not for me?"

"It's not safe for both of us," replied Saahil, momentarily looking at Rhea from the corner of his eyes, which Rhea did not miss.

"Now that we are already here, I will show *didi* around. I have my face covered anyway, so no one will notice me, and I promise we'll run away in a few minutes," said Sania.

Saahil shook his head in disappointment, turned around, and returned to the children without replying. If he was stubborn, Sania was no less. Rhea wondered what his problem was and why he was arrogant, especially around her. And why was this snob teaching the children of a village?

"So this is his part-time job?" asked Rhea, thinking it was probably an excellent way of making a quick buck.

Sania giggled as she led Rhea back onto the unpaved path that snaked through the village.

"These people struggle to feed themselves, *didi*. They have no way to pay for their children's education. *Bhaiyya* does it out of the goodness of his heart," she said, looking into Rhea's eyes, holding a part of the hijab to cover her face.

A guy with suppressed anger teaches underprivileged kids for free because, in reality, he has a good heart. It was tough for Rhea to digest. Rhea considered herself an excellent judge of a person, and there was no way she would change her opinion about Saahil by this one observation. He could fool his sister, but not her. She was sure he had an ulterior motive.

"This place is nothing like you would have seen in Mumbai, *didi*. The people here have to fend for themselves. They are part of our country, but somehow our rules don't apply to them," said Sania.

"Why don't they just leave and settle somewhere else?" asked Rhea.

"The same reason I don't want to leave this town, my mother and brother," said Sania. This is their home. There is nowhere else they can go since they neither have the skills nor the means. From the time they are born, they are taught to live as outcasts, something they have adapted to so well that they can't think of living elsewhere."

How can people be so pathetic? According to Rhea, not the lack of skill but the lack of intent was responsible for this sort of life. All they had to do was make up their minds, and then everything would change for them. But she didn't want to contradict Sania and decided not to voice her opinion for a change. After all, Sania didn't want to leave the place as well.

As they walked along the winding path, Rhea saw the

single-storey mud-brick houses stacked next to each other like matchboxes. Ropes were drawn across wooden sticks in front of the homes, along which clothes were hung to dry. In front of some homes, women with slings around their waists carrying babies were cooking using firewood and earthen pots. She saw an elderly man sit sullenly on a *charpoy*. Initially, she thought he was staring at them, but after they passed, his eyes were still fixed at a distance, as if he was blind or paralyzed. Men in torn vests and dhotis did their business, chopping wood or adding bricks to the houses without casting them a second look. They came to the far end of the village, and Sania pointed out the fields that grew crops of wheat, barley, and apricots, which were the most common vegetation of the area but were now covered in snow. Sania informed her that the villagers sold farm produce in the marketplace of Ladakh, which was their chief source of income, and they all shared it.

In the distance, high in the mountains, Rhea saw a couple of Indian soldiers patrolling the border with rifles in hand. They were a part of the border security force, Sania told her. This was the closest she had been to seeing a soldier, and although they were so far away and were soldiers of her own country, it instilled a sense of fear and pride in her.

As the tour was coming to an end, Rhea's leg began to hurt again. Sania then led her into one of the abandoned houses in ruins. When Rhea went inside, she realized it was a small three-room structure, just like most of the other houses in the village. She sat on a rock inside and looked out of the hole in the wall, which was once a window. Children were playing outside, completely unaware of their poor living conditions. They were also unaware of the beautiful world outside the village and all the possibilities life had to offer. It reminded Rhea of when she was working at White Arc and how she was unaware of the world outside of the hospital. Her world had been limited to seeing patients, performing surgeries, and trying to be the best surgeon she could be. Suddenly, being in this village made her feel claustrophobic and miss her city life. She couldn't imagine living in a place like this where women didn't have toilets in their homes, men didn't know where their next meal would come from, and children couldn't afford education or medical facilities.

"Let's head back home," said Rhea more urgently than she intended to.

They began retracing their steps back to the little jungle on the outskirts of the village. This time, Rhea didn't look around as if she could insulate herself from her surroundings and poverty by not doing so. Just as she reached the village square, where Saahil was teaching the children, she stopped and watched him animatedly explain a simple mathematical problem to them. He appeared to be in stark contrast to how he usually was around her. He was animated, laughing, and engaging every child. She couldn't help but watch and stare.

"He's not as bad as you think he is, *didi*," said Sania, noticing Rhea's gaze on Saahil.

Rhea wanted to believe her, but something sinister about him was gnawing at her from within. She didn't know what it was and why she felt so, but she was sure he was dangerous and up to no good. For a moment, she pictured him with a gun, and the next minute, the thought was gone. She wondered why that thought had crept into her mind, especially when he was doing something as harmless as teaching children.

Saahil looked up, and their eyes met, and his face hardened again. The same scowl and expression of disapproval took over his face as it did every time. It was as if he had a switch that he could turn on and off whenever he wanted. She saw him open his mouth to admonish Sania again, but just as he was about to do so, she heard gunshots in the distance that echoed around the village. Saahil heard it too and immediately ignored her and diverted his attention to the children, whom he began hustling into a nearby stone structure almost as run down as the one she had just come out of. More shots rang out, and he called Sania urgently.

"Come on, *didi*, follow me," instructed Sania, who grabbed her by her good wrist and began running towards the house where Saahil was shuffling the kids. As Rhea ran, she saw the villagers scampering into their homes and bolting the doors shut. Once Saahil had pushed them into the tiny room, he closed the doors. Rhea and Sania sat on the dusty floor along with the kids. She realized she was breathing hard and didn't know if it was out of fear or because of the running. The shooting continued, and she felt a couple of bullets sizzle past them outside. She looked around the room and saw all the kids huddled together, and surprisingly, they didn't seem as scared as she expected them to be. A couple of them grinned at her while she was too afraid to smile. Saahil sat in a corner, lost in thought.

After what seemed like an eternity, the gunfire stopped, and Rhea heard the doors of the houses open one by one. As if on cue, Saahil stood up, opened the door, and the children rushed out. He also waited for Rhea and Sania to leave before closing the door behind them.

"What was that?" Rhea asked Sania, her voice sounding shaky to herself.

"That is the shelling between the Indian and Pakistani troops," said Sania. "It's a regular thing, nothing ordinary for these people."

"It's a regular thing, and it happens quite far away, high in the mountains, right?" asked Rhea, realizing why the children weren't terrified. "Then why do the people lock themselves inside the houses?"

"There have been instances of a stray bullet hitting villagers," said Sania solemnly.

So that was what she must've heard outside during the shelling. She shuddered to think what would happen if a bullet struck someone in those parts. By the time they crossed the jungle, waded across the river, and got to the highly incompetent Leh Medical Centre, surely they would have no chance to survive.

"Go home!" commanded Saahil to Sania, and she didn't argue this time.

Just as they were about to leave, two men in traditional brown Goncha attire that had seen better days, passed by. Their faces fell on Rhea and Sania, whose face was covered. They nodded without saying a word. They were about to walk away when they saw Saahil behind them.

"How many times do we have to tell you that you are not welcome in Tashkar," growled the old man with a thick handlebar moustache.

"I come here for the children," said Saahil defiantly, looking into the old man's eyes.

The old man spat on the ground to show his disapproval. He was tall and seemed well over sixty, but Rhea could see that he was tough, a man who had worked hard outdoors in his youth.

"And what makes you think our children need a traitor like you?" he asked.

Saahil did not respond. Instead, he stood silently,

immovable, rooted to the ground.

"Go to your homes and help your parents with their chores!" commanded the old man to the children. "No education in this world will help you survive in these parts. At least not the education this traitor is imparting."

The kids scampered away. Rhea found it funny that they were more scared of the old man than the bullets they had just heard.

"And you!" he said to Saahil, "Stay away from these parts. Your family has caused enough grief to everyone here."

After saying so, he walked away. Sania looked at her brother with melancholy, grabbed Rhea's hand, and hurriedly left the village.

"Who's that?" Rhea asked, struggling to keep pace with Sania.

"He's the village headman, *didi*," said Sania, "And yes, before you ask, he hates my brother enough to kill him."

Chapter Twelve

Rhea was writhing in pain on her bed at home in Mumbai. It felt like someone had stabbed her in the abdomen and was wringing the knife around her intestines. She couldn't remember what had happened or how she got there, but she couldn't dwell on those thoughts since the pain was excruciating. Her father was sitting by her side at the head of the bed, looking at her with concern.

"We will get you the best doctor we can, and you will soon feel better," he said reassuringly, patting her head and trying to put on a bold face.

"But I am the best doctor!" Rhea wanted to scream, but no voice would come out of her throat.

"None of this would have happened if you would have just stayed home and gotten married like I had advised you to," said her mother, who was weeping at the foot of the bed.

That doesn't make sense at any level, thought Rhea, but as usual, she neither had the energy nor the will to argue with her mother.

"We will do whatever it takes to ease your pain," said Dr Gupta, the MD of White Arc, "By fair means or foul."

Rhea tried to scream out again but failed. He was an orthopaedic surgeon who no longer operated on patients. *Why was he operating on her abdomen?* He was the last person she would trust her body with since he was the crook who was responsible for ruining her life.

"That won't be necessary since I will operate on you," came Dr Nathwani's ghostly voice. "I am the best. And by chance, if I fail, I will throw you under the bus and continue as if nothing happened."

Her eyes darted all around, but she couldn't find him. She wanted to tell him he wasn't the best; she was. She remembered him telling her that the hospital would throw her under the bus if she were caught cheating, but that didn't make sense here, just like her mother. And she knew he wanted to operate on her so he could get rid of her.

"Don't worry, Dr. Rhea. I will not operate on you, nor will Dr. Nathwani. We have someone better than both of us— the best surgeon in this hospital," said Dr. Gupta.

Rhea stopped trying to scream because she was relieved to hear that they would not operate on her. *But who was this new surgeon who was better than all of them?*

The next minute, everyone disappeared, and she found herself alone in an unfamiliar beeping room with an overhead light so bright that it blinded her. The walls were all made of shiny steel, and the coldness from them made her grit her teeth. There were IV cannulas attached to both her wrists, and she was still connected to the ventilator through the tube in her mouth.

It was the operation theatre in White Arc, and a familiar face materialized in front of her, but she couldn't remember who it was. He was dressed in blue scrubs and a surgical cap and smiled at her pleasantly.

"Don't worry, Dr. Rhea. I am the best surgeon in town, and you are in safe hands," he said.

It took her a few moments to register, but she recognized him. It was the same patient who had fallen off the building, brought by his mother, wife, and employer, on whom she had operated. The one who was responsible for her life turning upside down. *But how did he appear here suddenly, and more worryingly, how did he become her doctor?*

"You have appendicitis," he said with a smile. "This will be over in a jiffy."

Rhea was relieved to listen to his words, and his assurance dissipated all her pain and worries even though she wondered about his credentials. She waited while he put on his surgical gown and gloves. Once he had done so, he grabbed a bowl, dabbed a sponge, and painted her abdomen with a brown antiseptic liquid. She knew that he would next place the green drapes around her abdomen, which he did with such precision that it delighted her. She waited for him to pick up the scalpel and begin the surgery, but to her surprise, he walked over to the opposite end of the operation theatre and bent over. Rhea wondered what he was up to and lifted her head to get a better view. She saw him pick up something from the floor, and when he rose, a chill went up her spine, seeing what he was holding. He approached her, carrying a gun in each hand.

"As I said, this will be over in a jiffy," he said, grinning.

He pointed both the guns at her and began spraying her with bullets while Rhea screamed out her lungs through the tube.

She woke up with a start, drenched in sweat, gasping for air with Sania beside her, holding her by her shoulders with fear all over her face. It took Rhea a minute to realize that she was in Sania's room, in Leh, and not in an Operation theatre being shot by a dead patient.

"You had a nightmare, *didi*," said Sania, handing her a glass of water. "You were screaming in your sleep."

Rhea gulped the cold water, which soothed her

parched throat. She took a few minutes to compose herself and thanked Sania, assuring her she was okay. Sania went back to sleep next to her, but Rhea found it difficult to fall asleep the rest of the night.

#

The following day, Rhea woke up feeling just as terrible as she had felt after experiencing a nightmare on her Zanskar trek. She was not someone who usually had nightmares, and the one she had during her trip to Zanskar was the first one she had experienced in a long time. However, last night's nightmare was even more frightening. What scared her was that the events and details in the dream felt so real, and they were cantered around White Arc and all the people she despised.

She struggled out of her bed and swallowed an aspirin before breakfast, even though she knew she wasn't supposed to. She walked into the living room, which also served as a dining room. For a change, Saahil was present too, silently nibbling his breakfast at the tiny table, his grim demeanour making the atmosphere seem even worse to Rhea. If not for Sania's cheerfulness, Rhea felt like she was at a funeral home mourning someone's death. Rhea joined them and helped herself to the *roti* and curry. Sania spoke about what they should plan for the day energetically, but Rhea didn't have the strength to match her enthusiasm.

"How come you are home for breakfast, *bhaiyya*?" Sania asked Saahil, stealing Rhea's thoughts.

Shainaz woke up early as usual and was busy cooking at her next-door eatery, serving the customers who had arrived for breakfast. Rhea marvelled at her commitment to her job.

"For the past few days, the river has not frozen enough for the trek, so we had to call off the trek for the next week," Saahil said, tearing away the roti with both hands as if it were

107

Rhea's head.

"So you will accompany the tourist bus today?" asked Sania eagerly.

Like many other agencies, Saahil's agency organized tours around Leh Ladakh in addition to the trek. Rhea often wondered what the people of the region would have done if it were not a tourist destination. They would all struggle to make ends meet like the villagers of Tashkar.

"Yes," was his curt reply.

"Where to?" asked Sania, unable to contain her excitement.

"Shanti Stupa," replied Saahil.

"Can we join you?" asked Sania excitedly, leaning forward towards him.

"You have seen that place a million times," said Saahil, looking at her.

"Of course," replied Sania, making a face "I want to show Rhea *didi* the place," she said.

"Hmmm…" replied Saahil disinterestedly, finished his breakfast, and walked away.

Sania considered his response to be a positive one, but it only hurt Rhea's already bruised ego. It didn't help that she hadn't slept well too. *What did he think of himself?* She didn't need any favours from him. The only reason she had stayed back in their home was because Shainaz and Sania had insisted that she do so, and Rhea didn't want to break Sania's heart since she had grown fond of her. She could also visit any tourist places by herself without having to put up with his obnoxious behaviour, now that her wrist was no longer in a cast. She decided that after that day's trip, she would head back to her hotel and spend the rest of the week alone like she had planned. She would ask Sania to visit her at her hotel so she could spend time with her and avoid meeting Saahil.

"But first, we'll shop something for you, *didi,*" Sania interjected her thoughts.

"I don't need anything," replied Rhea confusedly.

Sania held her by her arm and walked her across the street into a shop selling traditional Indian attires.

"I think you should try Indian wear for a change, *didi,*" said Sania, blushing.

Rhea was taken aback by her suggestion. It had been years since she had draped a saree or a salwar kameez. At work, she always wore her trademark pants or skirt suit and jeans elsewhere.

"You will look amazing, *didi,*" Sania said

Rhea looked at her and couldn't help but smile at her earnestness. She agreed, and both of them browsed through several Indian attires. Finally, Sania chose one and insisted that Rhea try it out, even though Rhea was sceptical.

"Oh My God! You look like an angel!" Sania exclaimed when Rhea came out of the changing room.

She was dressed in a white lehenga that revealed her midriff. The borders of the long flared skirt and sleeves of the blouse were embroidered in gold. The hem of the blouse was adorned with tiny pearls. Sania hurriedly picked up a pair of fancy gold earrings and placed them at Rhea's ears.

"That completes the look," she said with a look of satisfaction.

Rhea looked at herself in the mirror. On one hand, she felt uncomfortable trying something different, but she also really liked what she saw and admired herself in the mirror.

Within an hour, Sania and Rhea got into the tempo traveller, waiting for them outside. Rhea entered the vehicle first, looked at the occupants, and was pleasantly surprised.

"Ohho madamji! So nice to see you again," said Surjith Singh, the *Sardarji* from the Zanskar trek.

He was sitting in the front row with his business partner, the rotund Anil Sharma. Rhea's face lit up when she saw *Sardarji* dressed in a bright yellow shirt, red track pants, and a red turban, standing respectfully with hands joined, which she reciprocated with a grin. As she made her way through the aisle, the college boys from the trek hi-fived her one by one while she occupied the back seat where Divya and Prashanth were seated. Rhea introduced Sania to them, who also sat beside her. It was as if she had reconnected with her long-lost friends.

"How are you doing, Rhea?" asked Divya, holding her wrist. "We were so worried about you. Your fall terrified us all."

"I am much better now," said Rhea, showing the sutured gash on her forehead, which was healing well.

"All thanks to the team leader," said Prashanth. "I have no idea how he carried you all by himself on that slippery ice to the medical centre."

Till Prashanth had broached the subject, she had made a conscious effort not to recall the day of her fall. Prashanth was right; it wouldn't have been easy to carry her since she remembered how difficult it was to walk on the frozen river during the trek. She watched Saahil seated in the front seat of the tempo traveller sullenly next to the driver as Divya explained to her how he had administered first aid and then carried her almost 2 km in his arms while she was unconscious.

"Lucky you," teased Divya, elbowing her while Prashanth rolled his eyes in mock disgust.

If only they knew how much I hated him and how much

he loathed me. She ignored Saahil's dreary face and looked out the window at Leh's narrow, winding roads leading up to Shanti Stupa.

They travelled for about an hour, chatting and reliving the trek. *Sardarji* continued to regale them all with anecdotes of his life, which, whether true or not, fascinated them all. He even sang and broke into a *bhangra* with the college boys in the aisle of the moving vehicle. He tried to convince Rhea and Sania to join them, but both declined emphatically. It was just the sort of atmosphere that Rhea needed after her nightmare and sleepless night.

The sight of Shanti Stupa greeted them even before they arrived at the venue since it was visible high in the mountains from anywhere in Leh. But its magnificence struck Rhea only when she arrived on the stupa's premises. Once the tempo traveller stopped and she descended, it dawned on her that the stupa had been built on a raised platform, as if it served as an arena for the world to admire the grand monument.

Rhea walked towards the white and gold Stupa, soaking in its beauty. Several tourists were also gawking at the two-story structure.

"It was built by the Japanese Buddhists in 1983 and completed in 1991," said Sania proudly, as if she owned it.

Rhea always noted a sense of pride whenever Sania described something about her hometown, as if she adored every aspect of Leh. According to her, there was nothing negative about her hometown.

As they followed Sania, who had become their tour guide by default, they climbed the bare stone stairs carved into the mountain to reach the first level of the stupa. There, they were greeted by the sight of the Dharma chakra. Afterward, they proceeded to the second level, where there was a mural depicting a golden Buddha within a turning wheel of Dharma.

"This was built to commemorate 2500 years of Buddhism, right?" asked Divya, looking at Sania.

"Yes!" responded Sania, impressed that Divya had done her homework and then explained the monument's importance to everyone. Rhea noticed that some tourists who didn't even belong to their tour group were also intently listening to her. Her knowledge of history and her eloquence impressed Rhea as Sania explained about the mural depicting the life and death of Buddha and his attainment of Nirvana.

Once they had scoured every aspect of the stupa, Rhea walked to the periphery of the platform on which it was built and looked around at the bird's-eye view of the entire city of Leh and the snow-capped Himalayas in the background. The skirt of her white lehenga fluttered in the breeze, and she tried her best to reign in her hair, blowing across her face. She had seen such a scene only in the movies, which made her realize she had not watched one in a long time. Sania joined her but allowed Rhea to enjoy the serenity of the place in silence.

The beautiful sight of the city of Ladakh, the peaceful atmosphere on the platform with the Shanti Stupa in the background, and the smell of brewing Kahwa tea somewhere on the premises all stirred something within Rhea. A thought lingered within her, which was gnawing at her ever since Sania had taken her to the village of Tashkar. She was not a person who indulged in other people's business, but with Sania, she seemed to develop a bond of comfort and friendship, so she didn't hesitate to talk to her.

"Can I ask you something, if you don't mind, Sania?" asked Rhea, leaning against the platform's railing.

"Of course, *didi*," replied Sania, turning towards her.

"Back at Tashkar, when the village headman said that

your family had caused them trouble, what exactly did he mean?" she asked.

Rhea watched Sania stir uncomfortably, something she rarely did otherwise. She looked at the ground as if contemplating an answer to Rhea's question. For some reason, she seemed to find it difficult to find the right words.

"The reason…" she began to say.

"Why does it matter to you what he meant?" thundered an angry voice behind them before Sania could complete her response.

Rhea and Sania turned around to look at a red-faced Saahil clenching his teeth angrily. His fair and handsome features had contorted into a monstrous look.

"I…" stammered Rhea.

"Who the hell are you to interfere in our family affairs?" spat out Saahil so loudly that the tourists around stopped looking at the stupa and stared at the trio.

Rhea was not the kind of person who would back down from a fight. The thought of being humiliated in front of a crowd by someone as lowly as a tour guide was unbearable to her. She had been tired of his attitude towards her since the day they met, and she would no longer remain silent. To make matters worse, she had not slept well the previous night, adding to her anger and frustration.

"What exactly is your problem?" Rhea roared back.

Saahil was momentarily taken aback by her response, but he regained his composure and was about to open his mouth to say something.

"Who do you think you are to talk to me like that?" asked Rhea, not allowing him to respond. "From day one, I have been trying to be cordial with you because your family has been kind to me, but you seem to take it as a sign of weakness. Do you think you can insult me, and I will take it lying down? I have shown far better people than you their place.”

Saahil laughed, a cruel, sarcastic laugh that confused Rhea.

“This is exactly why I despise people like you,” he said. “This is why I put up with all these people, even though I hate doing it,” he said, pointing to all the tourists.

“You people think you are superior and we are inferior. Just because you come here from big cities with job security, a big bank balance, and perfect living conditions, you think that we are dirt to trample upon and not at the same level as you.”

“I never said that,” replied Rhea.

“But that’s exactly what you meant,” retorted Saahil quickly.

“Is it my fault I was born in a city like Mumbai?” asked Rhea.

“Is it our fault that we were born here?” asked Saahil.

“It is not! But you are the one who is making it seem like a punishment,” she said, pointing a finger at him.

“I don’t have a problem being born here, madam,” said Saahil, swaying his hand as if swatting away a fly. “I have a problem with people like you who come here, shit in our city, treat us like slaves, and then go back, forgetting this place.”

“Nobody treats you like slaves. And what do you expect? This is not our home. We are tourists here and are bound to go back home at some point,” said Rhea.

“Yes, this is not your home! It never will be. You people will never leave the comforts of your lives. You want your lives to be perfect,” said Saahil.

“Do you think we don’t have problems in our lives?”

Rhea asked incredulously. Do you think we lead the most perfect lives?"

"What problems do you have? You only pretend to have problems which you come here to forget about. Real problems are those a woman has to face to open an eatery to look after her children. Real problems are those where children don't have education, and people don't know where their next meal will come from," said Saahil.

Rhea could not believe what she was hearing. At this point, she could not determine whether Saahil was arrogant or stupid. But whatever it was, he had managed to get on her nerves.

"What do you expect us to do?" asked Rhea. "Leave our jobs and sit here and serve the people of your land?" she asked, her arms flailing.

"No!" replied Saahil. "Don't leave your jobs. Just come here and help make a difference."

"I am already doing that," countered Rhea, now too angry to think clearly about what she was saying. "I am spending my hard-earned money so that your agency can make money and your family and employees can make a living."

She said it with the sole intention of hurting him for everything he had said to her. Saahil shook his head sideways and clapped dramatically.

"Thank you for doing us a favour," he said, smiling, sarcasm dripping from every word. "If not for people like you, there would be no hope for people like me."

Saying so, he walked away, leaving Rhea fuming. She could not believe she had been spoken to in such a manner, and now she couldn't wait to get back at him before she left Leh.

Chapter Thirteen

Rhea was furiously packing her bags as if stuffing all her items into them would soothe her anger. She couldn't believe nor accept the condescending manner in which Saahil had spoken to her at Shanti Stupa earlier that day. Nobody had ever dared to talk to her like that at White Arc. It was unacceptable to her that a simple tour guide would have the audacity to put her down, that too, in front of others. She didn't regret whatever she had said to him.

"*Didi*, please stay back. Please don't be angry. Forgive my brother. He has been through a lot and sometimes doesn't realize that what he says can hurt someone," she said, pleading, sitting at the edge of the bed.

"But that doesn't give him the right to speak to me like that," replied Rhea, continuing to pack her bags.

"I know, *didi*," replied Sania, joining her hands. "I apologize on his behalf."

"You shouldn't," said Rhea, pausing and looking at Sania, "You have done nothing wrong. And don't ever apologize for something you have not done, Sania. You don't owe anyone anything."

"Okay, *didi*. But please stay back," she continued pleading.

"I can't," replied Rhea. "Not after what happened today, Sania. Besides, I was never meant to stay here in the first place, remember?"

That didn't convince Sania at all. Rhea noticed tears rolling down her cheeks as she walked towards the living room. She felt terrible since Sania had always been friendly to her. From the day they met, she had always been ready to help and full of life. Rhea considered her a friend in this remote land, and Sania looked up to her, making her feel proud of herself. Sania returned to the bedroom with some cloth bags for the items Rhea had purchased during the visits to Shanti Stupa and Shey Palace.

"Okay, since it's already late tonight, I will stay the night and leave in the morning," said Rhea.

The transformation on Sania's face was magical. She wiped her tears, and a smile lit up her face.

"We can stay up all night and gossip *didi*," she said with a glint in her eye.

Rhea couldn't help but laugh. Not only did Sania believe that Rhea was young enough for her girl talk, but it also amused Rhea at how she derived pleasure from small joys in life like these. Back in Mumbai, Rhea didn't even have time to spend with her family and talk to them, and here, she was expected to gossip late into the night with a girl she had met just a week ago. But Rhea would not deny her since she had grown extremely fond of her.

That night, Rhea and Sania had dinner together as planned. Afterward, they sat by the window in Sania's room, which overlooked the street outside. They chatted while huddled beneath blankets, enjoying a glass of hot lime tea and a plate of momos. Shainaz had already gone to bed, and Saahil had not yet returned home after he had gone off with the tour bus earlier that evening. As they sat there, they watched the crowd on the streets gradually thinning out.

"So tell me, Sania," said Rhea, "What do you want to do in life?"

Rhea knew that Sania did not want to leave their town for higher studies or work since she did not want to leave her mother and brother. Sania was on vacation after completing class 12, and she was at a stage in life with endless possibilities, and Rhea was envious of her for that. She remembered herself as an eager-eyed girl, full of life, studying in school and college. She participated actively in cultural activities, always taking advantage of the opportunity to get on stage for debates, speeches, etc. She was known as the firebrand with an unquenchable thirst for victory. Although many classmates detested her for it, she never cared about what people thought of her. Once she joined medicine, she gave up everything and focused solely on studying to become the best surgeon she could be.

"I don't know, *didi*. Probably get married and have kids," Sania said nonchalantly.

Rhea was appalled by her answer.

"Marriage and children do not have to define a woman's life, but can be a part of it," said Rhea.

"But that's not how it is in these parts, *didi*. The expectations around here are different. If a girl doesn't get married at the right age, it is assumed that there is something wrong with her or that she is having an affair," she said.

"Why should you follow society's norms? And why should you care about what people think? After all, it's your life," asked Rhea.

"It's not about wanting to follow the rules *didi*, it's about the options available. You know my mother needs my help around the eatery. My brother is working hard from his side. Between all of this, we don't have the means for me to go to an unknown city for higher education. It is easy for me to say that I want to break the rules, but not so easy when it comes to being practical," she said.

Rhea tried her best to put herself in Sania's position but found it hard to accept her views. As she thought about her situation, she realized that her mindset played a crucial role. Rhea grew up in a competitive environment where her parents encouraged her to excel in anything she wanted to do, just like her brother. They provided them with the same incentives and opportunities to achieve their goals. Her never-say-die attitude was instilled in her by her parents, and she was grateful for that. On the other hand, Sania had a different upbringing, making it difficult for her to imagine the vast opportunities in life that Rhea could envision for herself. If Rhea were in Sania's position, she would have tried to leave Leh and establish herself as soon as possible.

"If not marriage and kids, then what would you have liked to do?" asked Rhea.

"Hmm…" said Sania as she bit her lip, thinking about Rhea's question. "I always wanted to be bold enough to speak in front of millions like a news reader."

Rhea laughed. She was a little girl with big dreams. And there was no harm in dreaming.

"You are a bright young girl, Sania. You will someday achieve whatever you set out to do," said Rhea.

That brought a smile to Sania's face—the same infectious smile that Rhea had come to adore. She didn't want to dampen Sania's idea of a girl's night out, so she changed their conversation.

"So, do you have a boyfriend?" asked Rhea, and Sania blushed hearing the question.

"Aha!" Rhea said dramatically, "So there is a boy."

"No, no, *didi*," blushed Sania. "There is no boy. I mean, there is a boy, but there is nothing between us."

Sania's cheeks had turned beet red, which made her look even more beautiful in the moonlight shining through the window. Rhea wondered when was the last time she had a crush. She couldn't recall having one during medical school since she was always studying. After college, she had been more focused on her surgeries than men. However, she remembered having a crush when she was around the same age as Sania, almost 15 years ago. *Was it normal not to have been attracted to anyone for so long?*

She was about to ask Sania more about the boy when she looked out the window and saw Saahil enter the house. Her gaze involuntarily moved to the clock inside the room, which said it was 1:15 AM. In the four days she had been at the house, Rhea was unaware of Saahil's timings. The moment she saw him, all the animosity of earlier that evening came flooding back to her.

"Your brother comes home pretty late, doesn't he?" asked Rhea.

Sania nodded in agreement. They heard him walk into the nearby kitchen, and the faint sound of drawers being opened could be heard through the thin walls. At that moment, no one was on the street outside, and the house was silent. The slightest sound of spoons and knives being disturbed in the drawer was magnified. Rhea and Sania were sitting in the dark, so he didn't know they were awake.

Suddenly, they heard him leave the room and were surprised to hear the door outside open and close. Rhea saw him walking stealthily in the dark streets through the window but noticed something in his hand that caught a stray streak of light and glinted in the dark. This made the hair on the back of her neck stand straight.

Rhea looked at Sania in surprise, whose expression confirmed to Rhea that she, too, had seen what Saahil was putting in his pocket.

"Why is your brother carrying a knife in the middle of the night?" asked Rhea.

"I don't know, *didi*," replied Sania, fear written all over her face.

Curiosity stoked a fire within Rhea for the first time, and she wanted to follow Saahil to find out what he was up to. She realized that she hated him and that hatred had roots in how he behaved, which also convinced Rhea that he was up to no good. She always suspected something sinister in him. It was the exact reason the village headman asked him to stay away from the village of Tashkar. If she could find out what he was doing, she could get back at him for the way he had insulted her.

"Come, let's follow him and see what he is up to," said Rhea.

Sania looked at her, stunned. Going out into the streets so late at night without a male escort was unimaginable to her. Before she could refuse, Rhea was already changing into warmer clothes and boots, and Sania had no choice but to follow her since she didn't want her to go alone.

Within no time, they were on the dark, frosty street, trudging along at a safe distance behind Saahil. Rhea's suspicions about him were escalating by the minute. If running out of the house late at night carrying a knife was not enough, he was hurrying along the deserted street as if he was guilty about something. *What sort of business was he into that involved venturing into the night with a knife?* She shivered both at the thought and also because of the cold. Sania followed like an obedient student without saying a word, but Rhea could sense her apprehension. They kept walking for about half an hour, and Rhea realized they were heading to the village of Tashkar. Twice, Saahil turned around to make sure that he was not being trailed and, on not spotting anyone, hurried along.

Finally, he stopped at the river bank, where they had to wade the river to reach the mangrove trees leading to the village of Tashkar. Rhea doubled over with her hands on her knees, gasping for breath. She didn't have a watch on, so she didn't know how long they had been walking, but it almost seemed like a trek on the Zanskar.

"Are you okay, *didi*?" Sania asked worriedly, holding her arm.

"I am fine," whispered Rhea, her eyes searching for Saahil but unable to find him. It was as if he had vanished into thin air. Her sprained leg hurt, but she had almost forgotten about it.

Rhea began panicking. *How could he disappear into thin, cold air?* She looked around the dark river bank. Except for the trees swaying in the breeze, there was no movement. She heard what sounded like a single frog croaking in the distance. Rhea felt Sania's cold hands clasp her arms, betraying her fear.

"What are you both doing here?" they heard a voice behind them.

Both of them spun around and saw Saahil standing there with a knife drawn in his right hand, a menacing look on his face and bloodshot eyes. For the first time, he looked like a killer to Rhea.

"*Bhaiyya...*" started Sania, but he pointed his palm at her, indicating her to be quiet.

"What is it with you? Why can't you mind your own business?" he asked Rhea in a cold, calm, menacing voice as if a hunter was stalking its prey.

Rhea was too shaken by his appearance to formulate an answer. *Was this his plan to draw her out of the house?* Did he know that they were following him all along? Did he hate her enough to want to kill her?

Before she could answer, she saw his eyes widen, and he began running towards her with the knife. Rhea wanted to scream out, but her voice seemed to be stuck in her throat, just like in her nightmare. This was not how she had imagined dying, to be stabbed in an alien land by a stranger for no apparent reason.

Saahil reached her and caught her shoulder with his free arm. She was too dazed to resist and stood limply like a lifeless mannequin. *Now, I need not worry about my future* was the last thought that came to her mind before she was pushed to the ground.

Chapter Fourteen

Rhea waited for the knife to pierce her abdomen, for the pain to surge through her entire body, and for the warm blood to flow into her palms. Instead, she was pushed aside, which caused her to fall and strike her head against a rock on the ground. She opened her eyes as the warm blood that was supposed to ooze out of her abdomen streaked from the side of her forehead and saw Saahil ignoring her and running in the darkness towards the river.

Rhea was disoriented and unable to comprehend what was happening. She stood up, pressing her hand to the side of her head to stem the bleeding, and strained her eyes to see in the darkness. That's when she noticed an old man approaching the boat on the riverbank to cross over to the other side, with Saahil in hot pursuit. Rhea took Sania's hand and hurried after them, hoping to get a better look at the person Saahil was chasing. As they drew closer, Rhea realized it was the village headman and that Saahil was dangerously close to him with a knife.

Rhea was overcome with fear, gasping for air. She began shouting to get the headman's attention, but the flowing river muffled her voice, and her footsteps were too quiet to be heard. Adding to the difficulty, the headman wore a muffler to protect him from the cold, covering his ears. Rhea desperately grabbed a stone from the ground and threw it towards him, but it fell short, and she was left feeling helpless.

"Your brother is going to kill him," she said to Sania.

124

"He would never do such a thing *didi*," she replied, but Rhea could see the fear and confusion in her eyes.

Just then, to Rhea's amazement, Saahil changed his direction as if something had caught his attention and started running back toward them. *What is wrong with him?* It was as if he was running around in circles. As he was charging in their direction, she saw that his eyes were not focused on them but to their left. Rhea followed his gaze and noticed some movement in the bushes a little distance away. Rhea stopped, looked as two hooded figures emerged from the bushes, and charged toward Saahil, realizing he was coming for them. Rhea grabbed Sania's hand and continued running towards the headman when she saw them take out knives of their own, and the two of them clashed with Saahil. Sania let out a piercing cry when she saw the knives glinting in the moonlight, so loud and terrifying that they seemed to rise above the roaring river. By then, they had almost reached the headman, who turned around in alarm, hearing Sania's cries.

He looked at Rhea, who pointed towards the melee and fell on the ground, gasping for air, completely spent. The village headman fished a revolver from his handbag and fired at the three fighting men. There was a pop, and she saw Saahil fall to the ground holding his leg while she heard Sania let out another blood-curdling scream. He fired again at the two other men, but they disappeared into the shrubbery.

Rhea was struggling to breathe; her lungs felt like they were on fire. She felt light-headed and couldn't tell if it was because of the bleeding from the side of her head, her exhaustion, or the shock of what she had just seen. And for the second time since arriving in Leh, she lost consciousness.

#

Rhea was sitting on a tattered brown rug in a small room, with her back to the bare brick wall. She was holding a white cloth to the wound on her head. Although the wound on her forehead was small and didn't require any stitches, she found it funny that she now had a gash on top of both her eyebrows. The room they were in belonged to the village headman, who Rhea now assumed to be a minimalist since his two-room house seemed to have only the bare necessities of everyday life. They were in a living room, bedroom, and kitchen all in one. It was barely the size of her living room in Mumbai, with no tables or chairs, and was equipped with only a mat to lie down on. This made Shainaz's moderate home seem palatial by comparison.

At one end of the room, Saahil sat on the floor next to a wooden stand with a few clothes hung on it, clutching his right leg, which was covered in a cloth bandage, which bothered Rhea since she couldn't wait for it to be dressed in a sterile dressing once they were back in Leh to prevent any infection. Shainaz was grim-faced beside him in her black burka, and Rhea watched in admiration as she had not shed a tear since she arrived. After ensuring that both her children were fine and that Rhea was not severely hurt, Shainaz had enquired why the three of them were at Tashkar at that unearthly hour and had been updated by the headman's wife on the events that had transpired. On the other hand, Sania was a mess and had been crying throughout, clutching Rhea's hand. The village headman sat near the door with his legs folded, and beside him stood his wife, who looked at the floor, not having spoken a word to anyone other than Shainaz since the time they had assembled.

The events of earlier that night came flooding back to Rhea. She remembered the scuffle between the two masked men and Saahil and how the village headman had fired a shot in their direction, which had hit Saahil. She found it remarkably irresponsible of him to shoot in the direction of the melee when a shot in the air would have sufficed to ward off the miscreants. She didn't know what happened next since she had lost consciousness, but she remembered opening her eyes and looking into the headman's weary eyes, who had sprinkled ice-cold water on her face. He then offered her the same to drink, which was so cold that she felt icicles flow down from her throat to her veins and into her body. She stood up gingerly and looked in the direction of where the scuffle had broken out and saw Sania clutching Saahil's leg as he writhed in pain. She recollected running towards them and bending down to examine Saahil's wound, which was caused by the bullet grazing the skin of his shin, which luckily missed the bone or a major blood vessel. She pulled Sania's brown hijab off her head and wrapped it tightly around his leg to stop the bleeding.

Upon hearing the gunshot, a group of villagers were alerted and waded across the river to investigate. Rhea was surprised to notice that despite the village headman's animosity towards Saahil, some villagers didn't share the same sentiment and had come to check on him. She also observed that those who went to check on the headman didn't bother about Saahil. This revealed that Saahil had both supporters and detractors among the villagers.

They were all bundled into two boats, and Sania requested someone alert Shainaz about the same since she would be terrified to see her children and Rhea missing when she woke up. When Shainaz was informed, she had been driven to Tashkar by Saahil's agency van, and they were all now seated silently, looking at each other. The rest of the villagers had been asked to return to their homes.

The tension in the air was palpable, and nobody seemed to want to make eye contact with the other person except the village headman.

"Why can't you mind your own business?" thundered the headman, looking at Saahil, who continued looking at the ground as if he had been hypnotized.

Rhea found it ironic that the headman was asking Saahil to mind his business just like Saahil did the same with her. His silence only seemed to infuriate the headman further.

"You and your family have been a curse to me and this village, and I don't know how to get rid of you," he said, every artery on his face pulsating with fury.

Sania began sobbing again silently while Saahil looked as impassive as ever. Shainaz looked into the distance with a glazed look as if she was carved out of stone. The village headman's statement didn't sit well with Rhea. She had experienced only benevolence and love from the family, even if she loathed Saahil.

"Why are you accusing him? He tried to warn you about the intruders and saved your life," said Rhea.

The headman turned to Rhea as if he was seeing her for the first time.

"And what makes you think you can interfere in the affairs of our village?" he asked her.

"I am not interfering in your village affairs. I am just requesting you not to make false allegations against my friends," Rhea replied defiantly.

She saw Saahil stir in surprise by her comment, but he pretended he could not hear the conversation. Obviously, the headman was not used to being spoken back to, especially by a woman. Like Saahil, he was not someone to keep quiet about it either.

"And what makes you think that he was not part of that group that hatched the plot in the first place?" the headman asked.

Rhea was surprised by his statement and, from the corner of her eye, saw Saahil look up with agony on his face.

"I saw him try his best to warn you. I saw him attack them before they could get to you," justified Rhea.

"Don't go by what you see, madam," mocked the headman. "A traitor's son will always be a traitor."

Saahil clenched his fist while Shainaz shut her eyes tightly as if shielding herself from the comment.

"This family has been solely responsible for the pain caused in this village, more than the pain of poverty or any other problems that they face every day," he said in disgust.

Rhea looked at Shainaz, Saahil, and Sania and waited for the trio to respond to the village headman's big allegation. But none of them said a word, which made her believe that something was amiss with the whole situation.

"I am very sure that he was not a part of the group that was planning to attack you," reaffirmed Rhea, unable to understand why she was defending Saahil.

"How can you say that with certainty, madam?" asked the headman. "What if the two masked goons had nothing to do with me and just had some hatred against him? They probably came to attack him when they saw him approach me with a knife. Or what if it was all staged to look like he was saving me to get into my good books?"

"Why would anyone do such a thing?" asked Rhea, wide-eyed.

"Because his father's blood runs in his veins," barked the headman and spat on the ground.

Again, the comment was met with stoic silence, except for Sania's silent sniffles. What had their father done to make the headman loathe them so much, and why weren't they speaking up for him?

"He is right. My husband was a traitor," Shainaz said in a firm voice from the other end of the room.

Her statement stunned Rhea, and she looked at Shainaz, who didn't meet her gaze. She seemed to be lost somewhere far away, relieving the past, a painful past. She saw a tear flow down her cheek, but she remained poker-faced.

"We lived in this village once upon a time, and that was our home," said Shainaz, pointing to a house adjacent to the headman's house, visible through the window. Despite the darkness outside, Rhea could see the unoccupied ramshackle house. It was the same house Sania, and she had rested in for a while when they visited the village for the first time. Rhea wondered why Sania had not mentioned this when she had shown her around. Shainaz didn't miss the look on her face.

"Sania probably didn't tell you this because she, too, is ashamed of what had happened. My children are innocent victims of the heinous crimes of my husband," said Shainaz.

Her statement sounded ominous to Rhea. *Was he a thief who stole from the villagers?*

"We all lived here as one big happy family. Every member of this village was like a part of our extended family. There was so much poverty here, but Sania and Saahil were the only kids in the village who could afford to study in the school in Leh. We had enough money to lead a comfortable life, or at least as comfortable as possible in these parts," she said.

Sania continued to sniffle, and Saahil was quiet as usual.

"My husband worked in a water mill right on the border, and it never occurred to me how he made more money than the rest of the villagers. I assumed it was because he worked hard since he would leave early in the morning and arrive late at night," she said, her voice palpably heavy.

"Then exactly 12 years ago, in the dead of the night, he arrived here with two guns and entered as many homes as he could and began firing indiscriminately. He killed over 30 people in one night," she said, bowing her head for the first time as if she could not bear the burden of the words she was saying.

Rhea was too shocked. *What could have motivated a man to cause such a massacre?* Saahil stood gingerly and limped out of the house, not wanting to listen further.

"But why?" asked Rhea incredulously.

"Because we were unaware that the water mill that my husband was working at was a front for the place where people were being brainwashed to join the terrorist outfits across the border. My husband was one among them and was tasked to kill the headman and spread terror across the village of Tashkar," she said.

"Unfortunately, I survived," said the headman, his eyes as hard as a stone. "But not many of my villagers. And my two teenage children."

Rhea gasped, covering her mouth with her hands. The headman's hatred towards the family, the villagers' mixed reactions towards Saahil, and Shainaz's unwillingness to contradict any of the headman's statements all made sense to Rhea now. Losing both his children to a madman—w*hat could be worse?*

"What was worse was that I considered him my brother and had asked him to look after my family in case anything ever happened to me," he said as if reading Rhea's thoughts.

"My husband disappeared that night and was never

seen again. Some said that he had defected to the other side of the border. Others said that the border security force killed him, but if he was, his body never surfaced. After the massacre, we were asked to leave the village by the village elders." she said, looking at the headman.

The headman looked at Shainaz for the first time, and Rhea detected a hint of sympathy for her in his eyes.

"It was not easy to throw your sister out of the village," he said, his features hardening after a brief moment of showing emotion. "But justice had to be served."

Rhea's head spun with all the information she had just received, which overwhelmed her. Shainaz was the headman's sister, and her husband had massacred his family along with many other families of the village. It explained a lot. Rhea shut her eyes and realized that she was exhausted.

#

Rhea woke up with a throbbing headache. She checked her wristwatch and was surprised to see it was 2:30 PM. By the time she had arrived at Sania's house after the late-night adventure, it was the wee hours of the morning, and only when she laid down on the bed did she realize that she was utterly exhausted. Not only had she not slept that night, but she hadn't been able to sleep the previous night as well after her nightmare. The moment she had closed her eyes, she had fallen asleep.

Once awake, she sat up straight on her bed, and her mind went through the previous night's events. Now that she had the time to process all the information, she realized the magnitude of strength displayed by Shainaz and her small family. She tried to imagine Shainaz's agony at finding out that she had been living with a terrorist for a husband. The anguish of having that husband massacre her brother's children and innocent people of the village of Tashkar. She marvelled at her bravery. After being asked to leave the village by her brother, she set up a successful business all by herself to look after her family. Unlike her, Shainaz was not loud-spoken. She did not speak to people with a vengeance, but that did not mean that she didn't have that fire within her. This was a revelation for Rhea, since until then, she believed that the ultimate show of power was to be in someone's face all the time and show one's authority with little regard for other people's feelings.

Rhea was impressed by Saahil and Sania's resilience. Despite being referred to as a traitor's children, Sania never let it show and maintained a cheerful disposition. On the other hand, Saahil went back to the village to help the people as if he owed them, even though he didn't. This explained Saahil's grim demeanour and partly explained his tirade against Rhea at Shanti Stupa, although she still didn't agree with everything he had said. They both showed strength beyond Rhea's expectations. Being from a world where dominance was measured by the size of one's paycheque, this kind of strength was alien to her.

Thinking about her pay cheque drew her thoughts back to White Arc and her future. The past two weeks had made her forget her life back home. Once she got back to Mumbai, she didn't know what she was going to do since she couldn't practice medicine for a year, and she knew nothing in life besides surgery. She had saved enough to survive a few years without a job but was not used to sitting idle. Additionally, the thought of being stuck in the house with her mother constantly reminding her to get married was repulsive. Rhea could picture her mother bombarding her with one proposal after another until Rhea had no choice but to relent just to make her stop. She had nothing against marriage and wanted to settle down and have a family sometime in the future without compromising her career. But she didn't want to do it now, at a stage in her career where she was helpless, as a means of escaping the void her life had fallen into. The thought of going back home suddenly seemed repugnant.

After contemplating for a while, she finally made a decision. She reached out for her phone, which she had rarely used since her arrival in Leh, except for taking photos, and dialled her home number in Mumbai. On the third ring, her father answered the call. They talked for a long time, and she shared details about all the places she had visited, excluding the previous night's events and her fall during the Zanskar trek. After she finished speaking, there was a moment of silence between them.

"What is the real reason for calling *beta*?" asked her father, as usual, reading her thoughts.

He had this uncanny knack of always knowing everything about her. She detected a smile while he spoke.

"Dad, I have decided to stay back for a couple more weeks," she said.

"Have you found a reason to stay?" he asked with a smile.

"I don't know, dad. But I hope to find out," she said.

Chapter Fifteen

Rhea placed her clothes neatly in the tiny wooden cupboard of the colourful, three-storied brick hotel room she had checked into when she had arrived in Leh. The friendly, stooping Tibetan proprietor was delighted to see her back and was even more excited when she handed him her advance rent for the next two weeks. When Rhea revealed to Shainaz and Sania that she would stay back in Leh but move out of their home back to her hotel, they were highly disappointed. They tried their best to convince her, but she refused since she didn't want to impose on them. Sania, who was now helping her out with the unpacking along with her non-stop chatter, was convinced about Rhea moving out with the offer that she could stay with Rhea in the hotel whenever she wanted to have her girl's night out.

"So what do you want to do, *didi*?" asked Sania once they had finished setting up Rhea's room.

"I want to visit the village of Tashkar," said Rhea.

Rhea saw Sania's hesitation. After all, they had just had an unpleasant experience at the village, which resulted in Rhea now knowing their ugly family history. Sania expected Rhea to visit the city of Leh, Ladakh, to explore more tourist destinations.

"Don't worry about the past. You have done nothing wrong," said Rhea, patting her head. "Besides, I thought we could visit the village and teach the kids something."

Sania's eyes opened wide in surprise, and Rhea could not help but laugh.

"I am just in the mood to teach, Sania," she said, placing her hand on Sania's shoulder. "We should be able to teach those kids something, right?"

"We?" asked Sania.

"Of course," replied Rhea, "Both of us."

"I can't, *didi*. I am too afraid to stand in front of an audience," said Sania, shaking her head.

"They are a bunch of little kids, Sania," Rhea said. "Why should you be afraid of them?"

"I freeze when there is a crowd *didi*. I can't do it," argued Sania.

"Nonsense," said Rhea. "By the way, what does your brother teach them besides mathematics?"

"I think he teaches them a bit of everything," she said. "But he teaches mathematics most often because he is very good at it."

"Hmm… It's one subject I cannot stand," said Rhea. "I can probably teach them about the human body and some biology."

"Oh, I am sure they would love it *didi*. Nobody would have ever told them how our body works," said Sania.

"Which is your favourite subject?" asked Rhea.

"History," pat came Sania's reply.

"Then you can teach them history," said Rhea emphatically.

Sania wasn't expecting that. She tried her best to convince Rhea that she wouldn't be able to go through it, saying she would pass out in front of the children, but Rhea was adamant, so she reluctantly agreed.

Rhea didn't know how she would begin her newfound mission of teaching the village children. She didn't want to go from house to house since she was a stranger and the villagers would be sceptical about her. Saahil was on a trek that Sania said would last two days, so they couldn't take his help either—*not that he would help*. Furthermore, they hadn't spoken at all after the incident.

Sania came up with a suggestion that initially sounded strange but ended up being the only feasible one for Rhea. Together, they made their way to Tashkar by wading across the river and walking through the mangrove trees. When they arrived at the village square, where the village elders usually gathered to discuss village affairs and where Saahil conducted his classes, they set up the blackboard on the platform. Rhea had purchased the blackboard on the way to the village since they didn't know where Saahil kept his. Once the board was set up, Sania sat on the ground and looked at the board while Rhea stood with a chalk in hand, waiting.

Initially, nothing happened, but gradually, one by one, the children started approaching them with curiosity and sat on the ground next to Sania. Within fifteen minutes, the news had spread, and almost twenty-five children between the ages of 5 and 16 were sitting wide-eyed in front of the new teacher in town. Rhea smiled amusedly as she saw men and women peering from their windows at the scene unfolding before them. It was clear that besides Saahil, no one had shown any interest in their children before.

After everyone had settled in, Rhea introduced herself and Sania. Then, she asked each child to introduce themselves. The impromptu introduction session turned out to be an ideal icebreaker since many kids were nervous about standing in front of everyone, just like Sania. Some of them blurted out their nicknames, forgot their ages, or even forgot their names, entertaining everyone.

Once the laughter died down, Rhea got into the teaching mode earnestly. Being fine-tuned to interacting only with adults, she initially found it hard to teach the children that, too, with such a variable age group. Then, as she went on, she realized that all she needed was to keep it simple since they knew so little, and she could start from scratch, treating them all as six-year-olds. So she began by teaching them the names of parts of the body, the vital organs, and their functions. She saw them gawk at her diagrams on the blackboard incredulously. There was a round of laughter from the boys and silent giggles from the girls when she drew the male and female sex organs, during which Sania buried herself behind her hijab in shame.

Rhea was amazed when she checked her watch and realized she had been speaking for over an hour. She remembered her MBBS days when her classmates would get restless within half an hour into a lecture, but the children she spoke to were listening to her with undivided attention, not even stirring. She was intrigued by how readily a child's mind absorbed information, which appeared to vanish in adults due to the mistaken belief that they already knew everything.

Once done, Rhea offered the stage to Sania, who initially refused to leave her seat from the back of the class but was helpless once 25 pairs of eyes looked back at her expectantly. She stood up and took an age to walk to the front of the class as Rhea stuck her tongue out at her.

"I can't do this *didi,*" she whispered to Rhea once she reached her.

"You better do it," Rhea said, patting her back. "If you

don't, you won't be my sidekick from tomorrow onwards."

Rhea laughed at Sania's helpless expression on being blackmailed and walked to the back of the class. She began disastrously as she stammered and fumbled for words, and the kids giggled amusedly. But with every passing minute, her confidence started to rise. She was talking about the *First Battle of Panipat*. History and mathematics were Rhea's weak suit, and she couldn't recollect anything, even though Sania told the kids that it was one of the most famous battles in Indian history. Rhea was engrossed as Sania spoke eloquently about the war between Babur and the Lodi dynasty. She flailed her arms excitedly as she explained how Ibrahim Lodi, the Sultan of Delhi, was cheated by his uncle Daulat Khan Lodi, who had offered his allegiance to the invading emperor Babur. She revealed how Babur had used tactical supremacy during the war to dig trenches covered by tree branches to stifle the Lodi army. Rhea could see the wonder in every child's eye when Sania told them how the Mughal army cannons scared the Lodi army elephants, trampling their own soldiers and causing them to lose the battle.

The girl who, just half an hour ago, was struggling to articulate herself was now expertly recounting past events. This was not only because her knowledge of history was strong but also because she had a natural talent for public speaking, which Rhea had first observed when the girl explained the history of the Shanti Stupa to the public during their visit with Saahil.

"Teaching history and the human body to underprivileged kids makes for a great story to share with friends back home," a voice behind Rhea startled her.

Rhea was taken aback when she turned around and saw the village headman, dressed in his customary brown goncha, standing and observing the events. She was unsure of how long he had been there and didn't fully comprehend the meaning behind his remark, but she guessed that he was probably pleased to witness the children acquiring new knowledge.

"Isn't it great to see their eyes sparkle as they take in all this information?" asked Rhea with a sparkle in her own eyes.

"What is the use of this information?" asked the headman abruptly. "Is it going to bring food to their table? Is this knowledge of Babur winning a war or knowing how the liver works ever going to help them in any way?"

Rhea was surprised by his negative attitude. For her, education was the basis of life. It was ingrained into her psyche that a well-educated person could achieve whatever they wanted. And here was this man denouncing education.

"You seem surprised by my opinion," looking at her stone-faced.

Rhea didn't know what she was supposed to answer. She looked back at the kids, eagerly absorbing all the information Sania was bestowing on them.

"Follow me," ordered the headman.

Rhea trailed behind him in silence, curious about his intentions. He led her down the same narrow, unpaved path she and Sania had taken on their first visit to the village. Along the way, she caught sight of two young men with logs of wood slung over their shoulders, which the headman informed her were chopped from the forests on the mountain. The men respectfully greeted the headman as they passed by. A few women could also be seen walking around with empty mud pots in their hands.

"They are on their way to the river to fetch water,"

said the headman to Rhea. "It might sound strange to you, but we don't have a water source in the village in summer except for the river we wade across to get here. In winter, we make do with glaciers."

Rhea was surprised by the information because she had always believed that the region of snow-capped mountains, the source of the river Indus that supplied water to a large part of the country, would be self-sufficient in terms of water resources.

The headman walked briskly, and Rhea struggled to keep up with the older man. They soon arrived at a part of the village that Sania had briefly shown her before. It was a vast stretch of land where several men and women worked with hand-pulled carts, ploughing through the fields and preparing them for sowing.

"This is the only source of income for this village and a means of sustenance. Wheat, barley, and apricots are grown here. The produce that is not used by the villagers is sold in the city markets." he said.

Rhea watched them work without any machinery. It was all manual labour without even cattle.

"We can cultivate the land only for four to six months a year. For the rest of the year, there will be no water. We don't have fertilizers to ensure healthy crops, nor do we have any modern equipment," said the headman.

"And to top it all off, this land does not officially belong to us. We are tenants here. One day, someone will say that we cannot live here and will have nothing to disprove them. The only reason we are living here is nobody else would want to inhabit this hostile place, and we have nowhere else to go," said the headman.

As he spoke, it slowly dawned on Rhea why he was

telling her all this.

"The children you teach won't benefit anything from the type of education you give them. You will be here for a couple of weeks. You will give them hope during that time, just like that wretched traitor's son does. Then you will go back home, leaving them behind to face the harsh realities of life here. A reality in which they are wanted by no one except their parents, a world of struggle to survive on their own where they will wonder where their next meal should come from, a world in which they don't even know which country they belong to," he said.

Rhea stood there stupefied at the enormity of what he was saying.

"And in that world, the conquest of Babur or the workings of the liver will make absolutely no difference to them," said the headman.

He then walked away, leaving Rhea rooted to the ground like a scarecrow on the field.

Chapter Sixteen

Rhea stood at the back of the open-air classroom at the village square as Sania spoke to the children about the *Indus Valley Civilisation*. It was a bright sunny morning, but there still was a chill in the air that never seemed to go away, and Rhea hugged the brown shawl she had wrapped around her pink kurta top and blue jeans. The children sat on the floor wearing wafer-thin old clothes and didn't seem to mind the cold. Sania was telling them about how superior the Indus Valley civilization was even though it existed centuries ago with its modern drainage systems, elaborate water supply, elegant brick houses, and beautiful handicrafts. It was ironic that the village in which the children lived had none of those amenities, and it almost seemed like they were the ones living in prehistoric times.

Rhea shifted her gaze to the audience with their backs turned to her. It had been three weeks since they began the classes, and their numbers increased daily. That was because several women now accompanied their children and sat with them. That allowed Rhea to speak to them about women's health, menstrual problems, breast examination, and other women-centric health issues. For Rhea, it was like a refresher course of her MBBS days since, after her specialization, it was the first time she was venturing into teaching something rather than just performing surgeries. For the women there, it was an eye-opener to learn the wonders of their bodies and hygiene, which until then was alien to them. They enjoyed the sessions so much that many would stay back for Sania's history classes while others were forced to leave to return to work.

Saahil had inadvertently stumbled in during one of the classes that Rhea and Sania were conducting, and after that, made sure not to turn up at the same time as them. His timings were haphazard anyway since it depended on his work schedule. He would ensure that he conducted his classes when they weren't around, usually in the evenings. He had yet to make any conversation with Rhea after the night the headman shot him, but Rhea could sense him being amicable whenever they came face to face, which wasn't the case earlier. She had seen the headman walk by a few times, but he never turned and looked in their direction, pretending they did not exist.

Once the day's classes were done, Rhea and Sania walked around the village, soaking in the atmosphere daily. The sight of children playing games with sticks and worn-out cycle tyres, women preparing dinner using earthen pots and fires outside their homes, and the elderly lying on charpoys and watching the proceedings would greet them. Tired men and women returning from the fields would offer them broad smiles and fruits and vegetables that they harvested, now getting used to the two women teaching their children. Rhea would remember the days at White Arc, where she worked from dawn to dusk, unable to make time for anything else. Time was money; back then, there always seemed to be a shortage of both. Suddenly, she appeared to be in a blissful world, being in the middle of nowhere without the basic amenities that she was accustomed to, and yet she seemed to be at peace with herself, something she could never achieve until then.

"*Didi*, you have just three more days left to go back home," said a crestfallen Sania during the stroll.

"You can't expect me to live here forever," said Rhea, pinching her arm.

But she had to admit she wasn't keen on returning home either.

"Why not?" asked Sania, rubbing her arm.

Rhea turned towards her to confirm whether she was being serious or it was a joke. When she saw the look of genuineness on her face, she was amused and touched by Sania's affection for her. Nobody other than her family had ever shown her that kind of love.

Before Rhea could respond, a piercing cry broke the silence in the air. Another scream of agony followed it, and then another. Rhea stared at Sania with a look of terror on her face.

"What was that?" she asked, grabbing Sania by her arm.

"I don't know *didi*," replied Sania, alarmed.

Both of them hurried together towards the cries. The closer they got, the louder the shrieks became, and the agony was palpable with every cry. Rhea was sure a stray bullet had shot someone, though they hadn't heard any shelling. When they arrived at the location, they saw several women seated outside a brick house, talking in whispers. The older women chatted and laughed nonchalantly while the younger ones looked concerned by the wailing from within the house. The scene baffled Rhea.

"What is happening?" asked Sania, a woman beside the house.

"A lady is giving birth to her first child," said the young woman.

Sania relaxed immediately and sat on a rock since she feared the worst, like Rhea. Rhea, though relieved, couldn't accept the fact that someone could give birth to a child in a desolate, run-down, unsterile environment like this one, and that too without the supervision of a doctor.

"I want to have a look inside," said Rhea.

Sania stiffened. A woman in labour was the last thing she wanted to see, and she sat unmoved.

"Don't act like a baby. Someday, you will deliver one, too," said Rhea, looking at Sania's reaction and pulling her along amidst Sania's protests.

When they entered the house, the scene that greeted her was one Rhea had never expected to see.

The *house* was a single windowless room designated for childbirth for the women of Tashkar. It was lit by two oil lamps hung from the roof at the centre, casting a dull yellow glow in the room. The walls of the room were covered with cow-dung cakes, as it was believed to ward off germs. In one corner was a woman lying on a cot made of bamboo and jute, still screaming, covered with a torn white sheet with blood stains which Rhea was not sure of being hers or that of the woman who had delivered before her. Four women were around her, and one was seated on the floor, fanning the flames boiling a pot of water. An elderly woman in a brown saree was sitting at the head of the bed, wiping the wailing woman's face with a wet cloth. Another woman sat on the cot next to the lady in labour, massaging her abdomen.

In the centre stood a short, plump, middle-aged lady in a bright red saree and a huge red *bindi* on her forehead. Her hair was made into a bun and tied with a red string. Smoke emanated from the beedi rolled in the corner of her mouth. Her dusky face showed an expression of not really wanting to be there. Rhea figured out she was the *dai* who performed deliveries in the village. Rhea watched as the dai dipped her hand with red bangles in a bowl of coconut oil and nonchalantly inserted her sausage-like fingers into the vagina of the lady lying on a cot, causing her to scream and let out another shrill cry.

"The baby will come out anytime," she said, pulling out her fingers and adjusting the beedi with the same hand.

Sania puked her breakfast, and all the women turned to look at her and smile. She ran out of the room embarrassed, but Rhea stood rooted in her place, which the other women didn't seem to mind, and in fact, they seemed to relish the attention they were garnering from the tourist. Rhea watched as the *dai* asked the lady sitting beside the woman to push the pregnant woman's belly from above as the baby's head slowly started appearing. The moment it happened, the woman helping seemed to get an extra shot of adrenaline, and she, along with the dai, pushed and pulled in tandem, much to Rhea's terror. At one point, the shoulder of the baby seemed to be stuck, but the *dai* expertly placed her right hand into the woman's vagina and, in one sweeping motion, pulled out the shoulder. Rhea shuddered and looked at the woman lying on the cot who had now passed out in pain.

When Rhea looked back down, the baby's legs were visible. The *dai* pulled out the baby and hung it upside down dangling it by its feet, whacked it hard on its buttocks and it cried, after which all the women looked up at the heavens in unison and prayed.

She then handed the baby to her helper and began pulling out the placenta, which was still attached to the baby's umbilical cord. Sania entered just then, saw the scene, puked once more, and fled the room once again. Once the placenta was out, the *dai* dipped a pair of scissors into the boiling water and then used it to cut off the umbilical cord and then applied cow dung to the umbilicus of the child where the cord was cut off.

Rhea, who had witnessed thousands of surgeries, performed hundreds herself, managed numerous complications, and believed that she had seen it all, walked out of the delivery *home* and hurled by the side of it.

#

"What did we just witness?" asked Rhea incredulously.

Sania and she were back at the village square, which was empty since the children had left. Both of them were sitting on the platform, reliving the scene of childbirth they had watched unfold before them a while ago.

"I didn't even see most of it, and yet I am shivering all over *didi*," said Sania, who had turned pale after vomiting multiple times.

"You look like you were the one who just gave birth," chuckled Rhea. "Remember you said that the only thing you wanted was to get married and have kids."

The look on Sania's face was enough to make her laugh, but Rhea didn't because she couldn't get over what she had just witnessed.

"How can a mother and child survive such woeful conditions?" asked Rhea.

"But they do survive, *didi*," said Sania. "How do you think I and all the village kids were born?"

Rhea recalled her days at White Arc Hospital and its delivery suite. It had a fancy name - *Mother and Child*. It also had a tagline, but Rhea couldn't recollect what it was since it didn't concern her speciality. Couples would pre-book the birthing suites the moment they conceived for fear of losing the suite to someone else nine months later when their baby would arrive. The regular monthly follow-ups were precise after registration because someone from the hospital would call and inform the mother about the same. At the time of delivery, they would usher the mother into specialized water baths where they would float her in warm water for a near-painless, normal delivery experience. If normal delivery wasn't possible, the best gynaecologists in pristine operation theatres performed C-sections followed by 24/7 nursing care. Experienced paediatricians, handled the infants and formula feeds were recommended from day one to make the child plump and healthy. Once the process was done, the couple would leave the hospital with the baby in a Mercedes car hired by the hospital. Of course, all of this came at a price, a price only the elite could afford.

In contrast, what she had just witnessed was downright unacceptable. A dark, humid room, beedi-toting *dai,* and unsterile equipment were the norm. Cow dung on the wall and cow dung on the baby didn't seem abnormal to anyone. Rhea couldn't imagine anyone wanting to give birth to a child there. She sat silently for a long time, thinking about the whole affair. Surely, there was something she could do to change the process of childbirth and make it healthier.

"Get up!" she instructed Sania suddenly after being silent for almost half an hour. "Go find the village kids."

"But I thought we were done with our classes for the day," said a confused Sania, who had dozed off.

"Let's teach them something a little different," Rhea grinned. "Once you find them, bring them to your old home."

Sania stood confused for a minute and then did as instructed since she knew Rhea always had a reason behind any instruction. Rhea walked to the run-down place next to the headman's house. She surveyed it to look for what was usable in the house. There were three tiny rooms, just like the homes in the rest of the village. She found it strange that the village headman let no one else occupy the house, even after he had banished his sister from the village. *Was it because he didn't want anyone to occupy the traitor's house, or was it because he still considered it his sister's home and didn't want anyone else to take her place?*

Rhea decided she would convert the house into a clinic for the village where one room would be allotted for normal deliveries, one for first aid, and one for someone to see patients.

Upon the children's arrival, she assigned them specific tasks. Some of them, including Sania, were tasked with cleaning up the clinic's premises, while the others were to clean up the interiors with Rhea. She also sent two older kids to the city's hardware store to purchase paintbrushes and two paint cans. The work commenced in all seriousness, and it took them the rest of the day to complete the dusting and cleaning. By evening, the house was free of cobwebs, anthills, and rusted metal window frames. The premises were cleared of weeds and bushes that had climbed up the outer walls of the house as well. Rhea was tired but content and thanked everyone, reminding them to return the next day after classes to continue painting the house.

After Rhea's classes, Sania and the children began the paint job the following day. Sania had pleaded with Rhea for the clinic to be painted pink the previous day, and Rhea hesitatingly agreed. A few of the older kids climbed up the roof and realigned the tiles, replacing the broken ones with the ones from their homes. By that evening, the clinic looked completely different from the ramshackle it was a few days ago. The kids gathered around, buzzing with excitement. They didn't know what would happen at the facility but were happy to contribute.

"Now, the most important part," said Rhea with her hands on her hips.

Sania looked at her confusedly.

"The medicines and medical supplies!" exclaimed Rhea, flicking Rhea's forehead with her finger. "What use is a clinic without the medicines."

Sania slapped her forehead in frustration. She then went with Rhea to the city, where they found a small pharmacy. Rhea started picking up essential oral antibiotics, cotton swabs, dressing materials, and injection vials. She continued rummaging through the store and bought almost half of its supplies.

The middle-aged man at the counter grinned and handed her the bill, the biggest one he had ever made out in his 20 years at the pharmacy.

"That is too much, *didi*," said Sania, catching a glimpse of the bill.

It was as much money as Rhea would have spent in a couple of days back in Mumbai on non-essential items.

"It's okay. It's never too much when it is for a good cause," Rhea heard herself say.

As they returned to the village, Rhea and Sania found a group of villagers gathered around the refurbished pink clinic. She initially thought the villagers might be angry about her intrusion into their private space. After all, she was making changes in their village without anyone's permission. However, as they approached, Rhea saw the awe on their faces. Two men wearing vests and dhoti approached them with folded hands and pointed at something in front of the house.

Rhea noticed a small wooden table, a chair, and a shelf placed there. Sania then asked the men what it was for.

"They say that they built it for the clinic after what their kids told them last night," said Sania to Rhea in awe.

The villagers' kind gesture touched Rhea deeply. She had not requested help, but the villagers decided to contribute in their own way. Rhea expressed her gratitude and, with the help of the villagers, organized the items into three different rooms. One of the villagers even offered to build a table for the third room in a few days after Rhea explained what it was for. Sania and Rhea then placed all the medicines they had purchased from the pharmacy onto the new shelf the villagers had built.

After completing their work, Rhea and, Sania and the villagers stood in front of the small medical facility and admired their accomplishment. For Rhea, it was akin to building a hospital, which gave her great satisfaction. An elderly woman who was so short that she barely reached Rhea's waist took hold of her hand in appreciation, tears in her eyes and a heart-warming smile that touched Rhea.

"We need to give it a name, *didi*," said Sania once the old lady left.

"Tashkar Clinic," said Rhea with a smile.

Sania loved the name. Nothing had ever been named after the village, so it sounded great. She told all the villagers that it would be called so, and though it made little difference to them, the villagers were happy to hear it.

After everyone had left, Rhea and Sania were the only ones remaining. Rhea took one last look at the beautiful pink house amid the otherwise dull and drab village and then turned around to leave. As she was leaving, she noticed the village headman staring at them with an expressionless face. Rhea approached him, hoping to finally satisfy him with what the clinic would provide the villagers.

"I hope this will help the villagers," said Rhea, walking up to him.

She remembered how he had told her about the problems in the village and that the type of education she was imparting would make no difference. However, the clinic was more than just education. It was for the welfare of the people and would have a positive impact.

"You built a clinic; that is great. Now all we have to do is identify a child and send him to medical school so that he can run this facility after ten years," he said gravely and walked away, leaving Rhea devoid of all the satisfaction she had felt some moments ago.

Chapter Seventeen

"Dad, I would like to say back a little longer." Rhea heard herself say on the phone.

It was the last day of her extended stay in Leh, and she was supposed to leave for home the next day. During her conversation with the headman, she realized that all the effort she had put into the Tashkar Clinic would go to waste if she left it to the villagers and went away. She hoped to train a few people, including Sania, in the basics of first aid so that they could run the clinic themselves. Finding a doctor to manage it would be difficult as the Leh Medical Centre itself needed more doctors, and this clinic was a non-paying job. She also needed to teach the *dai* the basics of performing deliveries in a sterile environment using appropriate equipment and without the *beedi*. This would take time, but she had no choice but to stay back. The silver lining was that she would have the opportunity to spend time with the children and teach them more. Moreover, she would have Sania for company, which lifted her spirits.

"Sure," said her ever-supportive father. "How much longer do you want to stay?"

"Has she lost her mind? She wants to stay back?" she heard her mother exclaim in the background.

"Convey my regards to Mom," said Rhea with a

giggle.

"You can do it yourself," her father said, guffawing.

"No, please don't give her the phone," Rhea panicked. "I don't want a lecture on marriage. And I don't know exactly when I will be back, Dad," she added.

"As long as you are happy with what you are doing there, don't think of coming back anytime soon," said her father.

Rhea was touched by how understanding she was. She told him about what she had been up to recently and how she had helped build the clinic at Tashkar. From their previous phone conversations, he knew how she was teaching the village children. She could sense the pride in his voice at what she was doing.

"There is no bigger joy in life than giving," he said. "Do whatever you can. If you need anything more, we are here to help."

"For now, I just need you to believe in me," said Rhea.

"You will do great things. All you needed was the right goal, and I think you have found yours."

Rhea was unsure about what he meant. *Was he suggesting that her job at White Arc, where she had respect and income, was not the right aspiration?* Numerous doctors were vying for her position, and she was lucky to have it. However, Rhea wanted to avoid delving into it with him, as she had work to do.

So Rhea thanked him and hung up. She was eager to chalk out her next course of action.

#

So the next day onwards, Rhea and Sania began their next modus operandi. Rhea set aside the evenings to run her clinic for the villagers. The timings were perfect because the mornings were allotted to teaching the children. The villagers would be busy in the mornings with their chores, and they were more likely to visit the clinic in the evening. Sania was happy to be her assistant, especially after Rhea told her she had indefinitely extended her stay in Leh.

They began by examining every child individually, looking for symptoms of cough, fever, and skin ailments for which Rhea prescribed the necessary medications. When word got out, the adults began approaching her with their ailments. A few days after the clinic began, a villager had a fall while chopping wood in the mountains and was brought to Rhea, who sutured his wound under local anaesthesia at the clinic amongst an audience of villagers who watched her work in awe. Rhea also trained a group of women to conduct deliveries in a sterile manner along with the *dai*, who was not allowed inside without putting off her beedi.

As time passed, Rhea began to find fulfilment in her work. She could see her positive impact on the lives of the villagers she treated. Those with minor illnesses who received treatment from her looked up to her with admiration and gratitude. When a young boy returned to her, showing that the wound from which she had removed a splinter had fully healed, Rhea was overjoyed. She felt the same happiness when an elderly woman returned to her, completely cured of her long-standing cough after taking the medication prescribed by Rhea. Rhea wanted to hug her in that moment.

Rhea recollected her days as an eager medical student long before becoming a cutthroat consultant at White Arc, where she and her batch mates would visit villages as a part of the community medicine postings. She remembered feeling appalled looking at the people's poor health and hygiene status and how she, along with her batch mates, had vowed to make a difference once they became consultants. They would go back to their hostels and plan what they could do for those people once they had finished their studies and would come up with innovative ideas. But as the years passed, those promises were long forgotten in the quest to be at the top of the rat race.

As the days went by, more and more villagers sought her advice, and the clinic became so popular that people outside the village approached the clinic for Rhea's consultation, which was a proud moment for the people of Tashkar. Before the arrival of the clinic, nobody had ever visited the village except for a curious tourist who stumbled upon it. However, once the clinic opened, it brought in more people from outside the village, causing a significant increase in activity. The villagers took advantage of this and began selling their farm produce on rugs on the clinic premises. In addition, the men and women started selling wooden toys, bangles, and other handcrafted items that they had never had the opportunity to sell before. The villagers became close with Rhea and Sania, often sitting and chatting with them about their lives and sharing their stories. As a result, the clinic became the village's hub.

A few weeks later, Rhea was surprised when she spotted Saahil carrying a cloth bag as he arrived at the clinic. He always avoided meeting her when she was present in the village. Saahil seemed nervous and looked around for Sania but couldn't find her. As he had no other option, he approached Rhea and handed over the cloth bag. He turned around and walked away without saying anything more.

"What is this?" asked Rhea.

"These are just some medical supplies I brought for the clinic," he said, turning around to look at her.

Gone was the hostility in his voice she had grown

accustomed to when they first met. She was touched by his gesture and admired how he always found a way to contribute to the village in some capacity. It was as though he felt compelled to give something back to the village folk for the suffering his father had caused them.

"Thank you," said Rhea. "It's very kind of you."

They both looked at each other awkwardly, unable to decide what to say next.

"*Ministerji* has come," said Sania, thankfully breaking the awkwardness.

Rhea and Saahil both looked up together. Saahil's frown was back on his face while listening to Sania's news. Rhea followed their gaze towards the cavalcade approaching them. Leading them was a middle-aged man with a bald pate and a pot belly panting and wiping sweat off his head with a white cloth. He was dressed in a white safari suit with buttons straining to contain his protuberant belly. Next to him was a girl, who Rhea gauged to be around 12 years old, dressed in a pink salwar kameez. She had a slender frame, fair skin, and braided hair that reached just a few inches above the ground. They were followed by about ten important-looking men, all dressed in white. Rhea saw a few from his cavalcade run to the villagers' homes and announce the minister's arrival.

"He is the MLA of our district, Bhadrapala Tsering, popularly known by everyone in this area as *Ministerji*," Sania said for Rhea's benefit.

"He has come for his election campaign," muttered Saahil more to himself than anyone else.

"Who is that little girl with him?" asked Rhea.

"That's his daughter and the apple of his eye," said Saahil, probably unaware that Rhea had asked the question because he was looking at the minister with hatred. "He takes her everywhere during his election campaigns to garner more votes."

Rhea was disgusted by what she heard, but she knew of far worse ways ministers fooled people and sought their votes.

In no time, the villagers had made their way from their homes and the fields and gathered in front of the cavalcade at the village square. The minister was helped onto the platform on which Rhea and Sania conducted their daily classes so everyone could see him. He waited for the village headman, who slowly approached them and was ushered to the front to stand beside the minister.

"My dear friends of Tashkar," said the minister, raising his arms towards them. "As you all know, elections are fast approaching, and I am contesting for my third term in this area. I have done much for your village in my present term and will continue if I am voted to power again."

There was complete silence amongst the villagers. No applause, no cheers, in fact, absolutely no response at all. The headman was staring into the distance, unmoved.

"I will provide electricity and light up this village. It will take time, but I will not give up. I have two of the most important goals for the village of Tashkar in my next term. First, a bridge across the river will be built so that people will no longer have to wade across the river to get to the city. And the second one is to provide pipelines to irrigate your fields," he declared emphatically, placing his arms on his hips to show the people that he meant business.

Again, the villagers stood there like they were made of stone. Someone watching the scene might have wondered if they understood a word of what the minister had just said.

"And I will rout out those people who come here to

destroy your crops, threaten your headman's life, and make your lives miserable. My name is Bhadrapala, which means protector of the good, and I will protect all the good people of Tashkar from those people," he said, pointing at the neighbouring countries to make it amply clear to whom he was referring.

"Same promises every election," said Saahil, anger writ large over his face.

The minister realized he was not getting the response he wanted and needed to do something about it. It was time to pull out the trump card.

"And, of course, to show my commitment to your village, I have something for you," he said with a smile.

Suddenly, his motley crew began handing out brown gunny bags to the villagers, creating a frenzy. The men and women who had been standing desolately suddenly found life and began clamouring for the bags.

"What is in those bags?" asked a surprised Rhea.

"Rice, pulses, grains," said Saahil, "Sometimes even money."

The minister finally seemed satisfied with the reaction and talked about what he would do for them if he was voted to power, though nobody listened to him as they were busy hauling the sacks back home.

The minister's daughter was one of the people distributing the sacks and was the only one who had seen the trio of Saahil, Sania, and Rhea standing in front of the clinic. She approached them with a warm smile and offered them a packet, which Saahil gruffly declined on their behalf. The girl didn't seem offended and instead stood staring at Rhea.

"I have never seen you here earlier *didi*," she said, addressing Rhea.

"Yes, I am new here," said Rhea with a smile.

The little girl's eyes fell on the refurbished clinic and the crudely painted board on top of the door, and her eyes instantly lit up.

"Are you a doctor?" she asked eagerly.

"Yes, I am a surgeon," replied Rhea.

Rhea saw the look of wonder in the girl's eyes on hearing the information.

"I want to become a doctor too someday," she said, clutching the packet to her chest.

"That is good," replied Rhea, warming up to the girl.

"Can I come here when you treat the villagers so I can learn something from you?" she asked.

"Of course," replied Rhea. "You are always welcome."

They saw her skip along happily back to the minister's cavalcade. Rhea saw the minister fold his hands and bid farewell to the headman, who did the same with an expressionless face. The group disappeared, and the village resumed its normalcy.

Just as she returned to the clinic, a thought struck Rhea.

"The minister promised the villagers many things if he was voted into power, right?" asked Rhea, looking at Sania and Saahil, who nodded in confirmation.

"But when you first showed me the village, you told me that it belongs to no one, as in the people here are not registered voters," Rhea said, looking at Sania.

"She was right. They are not registered voters," replied Saahil instead.

Rhea looked at him, confused.

"On election day, the villagers will be packed in buses

with fake voter IDs to vote on behalf of someone unable to vote or deceased," said Saahil.

"But that is fraud!" said Rhea flabbergasted.

"Yes, it is. But who is going to do anything about it?" asked Saahil.

"Why doesn't anyone report it to the authorities?" asked Rhea.

Saahil chortled as if Rhea had cracked a joke.

"Don't you think people have already tried it?" he asked. "Even I have tried to report it to the authorities. And then I realized that the ones we report it to are also hand in glove with these ministers. The villagers themselves want to be a part of it since they get freebies during the elections. Then, you might wonder why the other parties don't report the fraud because they know about it, too. That is because they do the same with the other villagers, and each is afraid that the fraud would be exposed if they reported the other."

Rhea knew that politics was a dirty game, but she was not aware of the level of corruption. *How can fraud of such magnanimity be accepted?* Just then, she saw the headman walk by, and something within Rhea ignited. Here was a man who pretended to be self-righteous. He questioned Saahil's motives behind teaching the village kids but encouraged his villagers to participate in the election shenanigans in return for freebies. *Who was he to point fingers at Shainaz, Saahil, and Sania when he himself stooped so low?* She stomped her way towards him and intercepted him.

"How does it feel to be a fraud?" asked Rhea, going back to being how she was at White Arc. *To hell with respect.*

The old man looked at her blankly, like he had stood next to the minister a while ago. If she thought he would lose his cool at her accusation, she was grossly mistaken. He said nothing and tried to pass her, but she didn't let him.

"You talk about the terrible living conditions of Tashkar's residents. You talk about tourists like me giving false hope to the people here. But you don't want to bring any change in this village. You are nothing but a glorified bootlicker."

Sania stood agape at what Rhea had just said,` but Saahil watched in admiration.

"And you think that if I go against the minister, things will change?" he spoke finally.

"Of course!" said Rhea. "You are the village headman. If anyone can make a change, it is you."

"I have been trying to make a change day after day all my life. But at some point, you realize things will never change here. Political parties will come and go, but we will remain here forever without any change. There won't be a bridge, neither will there be water or electricity. It's all a mirage. Yes, I let the villagers accept freebies in return for casting fake votes. The grains each household receives will probably last them for a month, which is more than they can ever hope for, and I will not be the one who takes it away from them. So, if I am a fraud for looking after my people, so be it. At least I am doing it for their benefit and not my own," he said and walked away.

Rhea watched his tired figure move away from her. He was not carrying a gunny bag, which meant he had not accepted the freebies the minister had just given away. *Who is right and who is wrong here?* The lines seemed to be completely blurred.

Chapter Eighteen

As Rhea was teaching the children the next day, she noticed two burly men in grey safari suits approaching them. She was alarmed to see one of them carrying a gun. Having enough experience now, she knew that nothing could be taken for granted in those parts, and anything was possible, no matter how absurd it might sound. Just when her mind was conjuring up different scary scenarios, she caught sight of a small, slender figure in a yellow-flowered, colourful salwar kameez following the men. It turned out to be the minister's daughter, who smiled at her and took her place on the floor at the back of the class, much to the disapproval of the musclemen who found it unacceptable that she was sitting on the floor with the village kids.

Once the class was over, Rhea walked over to the girl.

"What a pleasant surprise!" Rhea said, sitting beside her on the floor.

"I told you I would come, *didi*," she replied shyly.

"Yes, you did," said Rhea with a smile. "By the way, you never told me your name."

"My name is Tenzin," she said, joining her hands in a *namaste*.

She has been taught well, thought Rhea.

"And my name is Rhea," said Rhea, offering her hand, which Tenzin shook.

They looked over at the front of the class where Sania had begun her history lessons.

"Do you teach every day, *didi*?" asked Tenzin.

"Yes, we do," replied Rhea.

She then explained how they taught the children biology, mathematics, and history between Rhea, Saahil, and Sania. Tenzin listened to her wide-eyed. She was just thirteen but seemed to have a mature head on her shoulders.

"I am having my holidays, *didi*, and I would love to teach them my science lessons," Tenzin said.

Rhea was impressed that the little girl wanted to do something from her side and readily accepted her offer.

True to her word, Tenzin arrived every morning with her bodyguards and pink school bag, carrying her science textbooks. She joined Rhea and Sania in teaching the children, and the children immediately took a liking to her because they were in awe of such a young girl who knew so much. Her friendly and cheerful demeanour also helped create a bond with the children.

She taught them how to create a mini volcano using clay and paper, attach small stones to plastic bags to make parachutes, which they let down from the clinic's roof, and perform various other experiments from her science textbooks, explaining their principles. The children enjoyed this new dimension of teaching for the first time.

After the classes, Tenzin bombarded Rhea with questions about her profession, her surgeries, and her doubts about the medical profession. Rhea explained the same to her and watched Tenzin pick up all the information she offered.

She even helped with the clinic if anyone arrived in the mornings since her father did not allow her to visit the village in the evening. Tenzin became an integral part of the system, and the classes that Saahil initially started now had three additional teachers in Rhea, Sania, and Tenzin.

Rhea sat by the door, overlooking the bustling street where tourists and locals mingled. Watching the cobbled street filled with people buying, selling, and bargaining was her favourite pastime. Now that she was living in Leh, it had become customary for her to visit and stay with Sania whenever she was bored with her tiny hotel room. Shainaz and Sania were always happy to have her around, and now even Saahil welcomed her, though he spoke only when needed.

It was the weekend, and Rhea had planned to spend the night and leave the next day. It was late enough that the streets were becoming less crowded but not so late that the markets had completely shut down. She wrapped her arms around her knees to protect herself from the chill. She laughed, wondering how her two-week trip to Leh had turned into a three-month stay. Despite the challenges the place offered, she had enjoyed every minute of her time there, and it had flown by so quickly. Her life in Mumbai now seemed like a mirage, and she dreaded the thought of returning. The idea of working with cut-throat doctors like Dr. Gupta and Dr. Nathwani seemed repulsive. She couldn't believe how she worked day and night without sparing time for herself, without enjoying the small moments of life, keeping in touch with her friends, and without having a proper conversation with her family for days, even though they lived under the same roof.

Just as she was dwelling on these thoughts, she saw Saahil approach the house in a hurry. He stood still when he saw her at the entrance out of habit and because he had not expected her to be home that day. He smiled awkwardly, and so did Rhea. They were much more cordial than when she had just arrived, but he was still uncomfortable around her. She watched him dash into the house and hurry back out with a bag.

"Where are you off to?" asked Rhea.

He thought for a moment, contemplating a reply.

"To Tashkar," he said awkwardly, placing his backpack on his right shoulder.

Rhea glanced at her watch and noticed that it was almost 11 p.m.

"How come at this time?" asked Rhea. "I don't mind coming along since I have nothing to do here. Sania is busy, and *Shainaz's Kitchen* has a lot of customers today."

"I don't think you will enjoy it," he said more urgently than he wanted to.

"I enjoy every minute I spend in Tashkar, and the last time I came along, you got shot, remember? I can't miss that for anything," joked Rhea, which made even Saahil smile.

He reluctantly agreed. They got into the minivan, and he dropped his backpack onto the backseat and drove away. They reached in fifteen minutes, got off the minivan, and Saahil untied the boat anchored at the water's edge. Both of them got into the boat, and Saahil rowed them. By now, Rhea was freezing and regretted not wearing something warm.

"Whom do you teach at this hour?" Rhea asked as Saahil was wading them across the river.

"I am not here to teach anyone," he replied, not realizing she was joking.

"Are you here to meet a girl?" she teased him.

His cheeks turned a crimson red in the moonlight.

"No," he replied, not making eye contact with her.

"You talk very little if you don't have to abuse someone, right?" asked Rhea.

She saw him blush with embarrassment.

"I am very sorry for the way I behaved with you. I

misjudged you," he said, not making eye contact with her.

It was the first time he was apologizing to Rhea, and his gesture touched her.

"I am not sorry for how I behaved with you because you deserved it," she said.

Saahil laughed heartily, which made her feel at ease with him. When they reached the shore, he assisted her in disembarking from the boat and put his backpack on one shoulder. She followed him to the mangrove trees, anticipating they would walk down the small hill and enter the village. However, he stopped at the edge of the hillock.

"This is where we stop," he said, sitting on the ground.

Rhea decided to follow along, even though she couldn't understand why. From their elevated position, they had a clear view of the village of Tashkar below. She could see a few houses faintly illuminated by oil lamps, but the rest were shrouded in darkness, presumably because the villagers were all asleep.

Saahil opened his backpack and handed her a pair of binoculars.

"Look there," he said, pointing toward the fields.

Rhea did as she was told and looked but could see nothing except wheat and barley crops swaying lazily in the night air. She scanned the entire length of the field but could identify nothing out of place. A scarecrow stood in the middle of the field, its shirt fluttering in the breeze.

"I can't find…" she started saying, turning her gaze to Saahil, but froze when she saw him holding a sniper rifle.

"What the hell! Are you out of your mind?" she exclaimed, not believing what she saw.

Just when I was getting comfortable with him he whips out a gun.

"Don't worry; this is not my first time with a gun," he said calmly, which terrified her even more. "And I will not kill anyone."

Rhea was feeling extremely anxious and couldn't keep calm. It was the first time in her life that she had been so close to a gun. She couldn't even reprimand him as she had insisted on accompanying him. She was also unable to go back home without his assistance. Now, she wished that she had brought Sania along with her.

"You remember the minister telling the villagers that he would rid them of the miscreants who were targeting their crops, their lives, and the life of the headman as well?" asked Saahil, adjusting the sniper.

"Yes," said Rhea, not forgetting how the minister pointed at the mountains while saying so, reminding the villagers whom he was referring to.

"Those miscreants are none other than the minister's henchmen and not from some other country," said Saahil. "He sends them to the village to destroy the crops and threaten the headman's life."

"But what will he achieve by doing such a thing?" asked Rhea, unable to believe such an allegation even though she didn't like the minister.

"To instil fear," said Saahil angrily, looking at her. "He creates fear and then pretends to be the saviour who comes to their rescue."

"That is terrible," said Rhea. "Why doesn't anyone do something about it?"

Saahil laughed.

"If anyone could do something about it, do you think I would roam in the dead of night, rifle in hand?" Saahil asked.

Rhea understood what he meant. People in top

positions wielded all the power, and these villagers could do nothing about it. The poor people of the village believed whatever the minister told them because he gave them hope. And hope is something everyone latches onto in their lives, especially in these parts.

Saahil then instructed Rhea to keep a watch on the field with her binoculars as he watched through the scope of his sniper.

"What will you do if someone comes?" asked Rhea.

"Shoot them in the leg," said Saahil calmly, still looking through the scope. "That's the only way to fight fire with fire."

Rhea shivered, partly because of the cold and partly out of fear. *How could she justify shooting someone, being a doctor, being a human being?* But on the other hand, Saahil was trying to protect the villagers in the only way possible. *By fair means or foul,* the MD of White Arc's words reverberated in her ears. The same could be applied here, too, but could it be justified when it involved guns?

Both of them lay flat on the cold, bushy ground, keeping watch over the field. She could hear crickets stridulating around her as though waiting in anticipation. The ground's dampness slowly began to soak through her clothes, but Saahil remained focused. It wasn't long before she spotted movement amongst the wheat bushes. She squinted hard through her binoculars and, as Saahil had predicted, she saw five men wearing black hoodies and black scarves covering their faces, crawling in the dark with knives and axes. Rhea looked at Saahil, who was still watching through his sniper, wondering if he had spotted them.

"I see them," he said without looking at her.

She peered back into the binoculars as she saw the

men silently uproot the crops one by one. Saahil waited a few minutes to prove his statement to her. Rhea heard a click beside her, and the next moment, one man was clutching his leg and crying out in agony. She watched the other men look around in fear. They dropped their tools and carried the wounded man away. Then, it all became silent again.

#

"I will protect you all from the miscreants who are destroying your crops and making your lives miserable," the minister told the villagers.

Like last time, the villagers had gathered faithfully at the village square. Rhea, Saahil, and Sania watched from the clinic. Tenzin was with them, too, listening to her father speak on the platform. Saahil kicked the ground disgustedly, and Rhea couldn't blame him after what she had witnessed the previous week with him when the miscreants had tried to destroy the crops.

"I am sorry," said Saahil when he realized she was with them.

Rhea admired Saahil's character. He didn't take the minister's anger on his daughter. He seemed to understand that her father's misdemeanours were not hers. If only he realized that his father's faults were not his, and he didn't have to pay for them.

"It's okay," said Tenzin, softly.

They watched as the food grains were distributed again, which the villagers gleefully accepted. Once the spectacle concluded, the cavalcade started returning to the river. The minister looked around for his daughter from the platform and saw her standing with the trio at the clinic. He approached them with a broad grin.

"Hello, madamji," he said with his hands folded, his

171

bald pate shining in the sunlight, "My daughter seems to be an admirer of yours."

Rhea stood motionless without a smile on her face. Her lack of response perplexed the minister, especially since a few villagers were watching them.

"It's so nice of you to be doing something for the villagers," he said, looking behind her at the clinic.

"It would be nice if you tried to do the same," shot back Rhea.

It was not the response he was expecting, evident by how the smirk was wiped off his face. A minister in those parts was not accustomed to be questioned, and that too by a woman.

"What do you mean?" he asked.

"Instead of just empty promises, why don't you really provide them with water, electricity, and the damn bridge?" Rhea asked.

"I work day and night for these people," said the minister. "What will a tourist like you know how difficult it is to get things done here?"

Evidently, he had given up on the facade of being courteous with her.

"If you could get things done, you would have done it by now." Rhea retorted.

That infuriated the minister. Not only did this tourist have the gall to speak to him in such a manner, but she was also doing it in front of everyone.

"If it is that easy, why don't you do it yourself," snickered the minister.

He held his daughter's hand and walked away smiling, dragging her along.

"I should have told him about knowing what his men

did at the field," Rhea told Saahil and Sania once everyone had left.

"It's of no use. We have no proof," said Saahil. "And talking to him is like talking to a stupa made of ice. With such people, attack is the only form of defence."

All three walked back to the clinic, lost in their thoughts.

#

Rhea couldn't focus on anything else for the rest of the afternoon as the minister's words needled her throughout. Her patients came and went as she prescribed medications without her usual zeal. Sania tried to take Rhea's mind off what the minister had said, but she failed. *Why don't you do something about it yourself?* He had mocked her, and the words echoed around her, challenging her, taunting her. In reality, she knew that Tashkar was not her responsibility; she was, after all, just a tourist. But she had come to love the people there, and more importantly, she couldn't digest the fact that he had challenged her as if she was not capable of accepting it. Rhea never ran away from a fight.

Saahil asked her not to overthink it because, according to him, it was not worth it. He had been there all his life and knew how the system worked. He had described the minister as a stupa made of ice—cold, hard, and insensitive.

The term *stupa made of ice* somehow stuck in her head. It seemed to describe many people she knew, such as Mr Gupta, the MD of White Arc; Dr Nathwani, the senior gastro-surgeon; and Bhadrapala, the minister. The term sounded familiar as well. *Where else had she heard it?* She was sure that someone had spoken about it to her earlier. An *ice stupa* was what she had heard. When she racked her brain, it finally dawned on her that Divya had mentioned it during the Zanskar trip. She was muttering something about an ice stupa providing water in the arid lands of the northeast. Back then, Rhea had paid little attention to it since she was uninterested and more worried about surviving the trek than a lecture on ice stupas.

Suddenly, her interest in the topic was piqued, and she wanted to know more about these ice stupas. She wanted to talk to Divya but realized she didn't have her number.

"Do you keep a register with the numbers of all your clients?" asked Rhea urgently.

"Yes," replied Saahil, "In my office."

"Take me to your office right now," she commanded him, much to the astonishment of Saahil and Sania.

Chapter Nineteen

"Hi, Divya. How are you doing?" asked Rhea.

"Oh my God! What a pleasant surprise, Rhea!" said Divya on the phone. "I am fine, what about you?"

"I am fine, thank you. It's so nice to reconnect with you again. How is Prashanth? Did the honeymoon in Leh produce any results?" teased Rhea.

Divya burst out laughing.

"No, No… Leh was too cold to produce results," she giggled. "How is Mumbai?"

"I am still in Leh," said Rhea with a smile, and as expected, she was greeted with a gasp from Divya.

It had been five months since they last spoke to each other during the visit to Shanti Stupa. During the trek, Rhea told Divya she would be in Leh for two weeks and then return to Mumbai. She filled her in on what she had been up to in the past five months, how she had followed Saahil, and he had ended up getting shot in the leg, the way she began teaching the children of the village of Tashkar, how she refurbished the clinic at the village and her encounters with the minister. When she was done, she heard Divya whistle in admiration.

"You are truly an exceptional woman," said Divya.

"Thank you," said Rhea. "And there is something you can do for me."

"Fire away," she replied without hesitation.

"Remember, during the trek, you were talking about ice stupas. I wanted to know more about them," said Rhea.

"Oh yes," replied Divya, remembering their conversation during the morning walk at the Zanskar trek while searching for the makeshift restroom. "It was something I had come across while researching a project during my days as an architecture student. Ice Stupas are a system where water is frozen as mini mountains in winter, and they are then used in summer as water sources in areas where there is scarcity."

The concept intrigued Rhea, and she asked her for more details. Divya explained whatever she knew about it.

"Wow, that's really interesting," said Rhea thoughtfully after hearing everything Divya had to say about ice stupas.

"You called me from Leh just to improve your knowledge about ice stupas?" Divya asked, already guessing what she had in mind.

"Hmm…" mumbled Rhea, wondering if she would sound stupid if she told her what she had in mind.

"It will require someone with the knowledge of architecture, and it'll cost a few bucks as well," Divya volunteered when she saw Rhea hesitate.

"Yes, I know," said Rhea.

"I am ready to help you with whatever you have in mind," said Divya without waiting for Rhea to answer. "And I know someone else who would be ready to help."

#

"Madamji. Did you adopt Leh, or did Leh adopt you," said Surjith Singh, the *Sardarji*.

As usual, he was dressed in bright colours with a neon pink turban, yellow trousers, and a black T-shirt on which he had worn a flashy golden jacket. Rhea laughed and gave him a warm hug. Even though she had not known him for more than a few days, back when they spent time together on the trek and Shanti Stupa six months ago, she felt she was meeting a long-lost friend. Divya hugged him, too.

After their phone conversation three weeks ago, Divya had booked her tickets and flown to Leh as promised. She had also told Rhea she would approach someone else but hadn't disclosed who it was, and Rhea assumed it to be her husband, Prashanth. Only when Divya landed in Leh that morning did she reveal that she had contacted *Sardarji*, and he was enthusiastic enough to be a part of the project. The combination of his expertise in the construction industry and Divya's knowledge of architecture would be extremely valuable.

"I am so glad to see you," said Rhea, "And it is so kind of you to be a part of this project."

"I am just here to promote my business. I can tell everyone that my business has reached Leh," said *Sardarji*, poker-faced.

Everyone laughed. Since time was of the essence, they got to work immediately. After walking through the entire village, Divya informed them they could use the land next to the field to erect the stupa. Since the water would have to come from the river, she suggested they lay the pipelines high in the mountains from where the river flowed. Those pipes would end at the land next to the field, where they would create an artificial water body. Once the pipelines were laid, water would be pumped every night in winter, and that water would rise high through the exit pipe at the trench around which tree branches would be cut and placed. When it went high in the air, the water would freeze instantly because of the cold and slowly accumulate around the branches until it formed a mountain of ice, an *ice stupa*. When the temperatures rose in summer, the ice stupa would slowly melt and provide water.

"Ohho!" said *Sardarji*, "This is unbelievable."

"Yes!" added Sania

"Do you think it's possible?" asked Rhea, unsure after listening to the enormity of the plan.

"Of course, it is possible," said Divya confidently. However, we will need a lot of workforce."

"The entire village will provide the manpower we need; don't worry about that," Saahil assured.

Suddenly, the excitement was palpable in the air. Neither the villagers nor Rhea and her gang had ever been a part of a venture outside their comfort zone of this magnitude. Saahil gathered the villagers and explained the blueprint of the *ice stupa* and what was expected of them. They listened in wondrous amazement and immediately pledged their wholehearted support. It was decided that all the men would get to work at once. Saahil then accompanied *Sardarji* to the city, where they scouted for the needed equipment, like pipes, generators, etc.

It took a whole week for all the necessary equipment to arrive, and finally, the work began. Rhea had expected it to be challenging, but she had not anticipated how gruelling it would be. Saahil and *Sardarji*, along with Rhea, trekked to the mountain from where they would get the water for the stupa. It took them almost three hours to reach the spot on foot, and by then, the villagers had already started digging the earth to lay the pipes. Rhea watched *Sardarji* expertly guide them on what needed to be done, sometimes doing it himself when he couldn't get his message across to the villagers. The pipeline needed to be laid almost 4 km down the mountain to the trench beside the field being dug up by another group of villagers under Divya's guidance. The work was strenuous, but the thought of the outcome seemed to inspire everyone who was a part of it, and they gave it everything they had.

#

"It was so nice of Divya *didi* and *Sardarji* to come all the way here to help out with the ice stupa project, *didi*," said Sania.

The villagers had been working non-stop for over a month. Rhea and Sania were at the clinic, exhausted after walking around the fields following their morning classes. They checked every aspect of the work in progress every day. Divya and Sardarji had left a week after the work had begun since they had to return to their jobs, but they kept a close eye on what was happening in Tashkar. Rhea would video call them every morning and evening to show them the progress, and they would give instructions on what had to be done. Rhea felt like they were her new best friends, and she couldn't remember the last time she had a circle of friends like this.

"They insisted on sharing the costs as well, which is very generous of them," added Rhea, sincerely touched.

"How many more days do you think we'll need to finish it, *didi?*" Sania asked.

"The trench with the exit pipe and branches around it are ready," said Rhea. "I think it'll take a week or so for the pipeline to reach the trench."

Just as she spoke, she saw the minister's cavalcade enter the village. It had been quite some time since he had visited the village, probably assuming that the gunny bags he distributed last time would last a while, just as the headman had informed her. Now that the elections were approaching, she expected his visits to become more frequent. She saw him prance across the village along with Tenzin, who broke away from the troop and joined Rhea when she spotted her.

179

"How are you, Rhea *didi*?" asked Tenzin excitedly.

"I am fine, thank you, Tenzin," said Rhea, patting her head. "I am seeing you in Tashkar after a long time?"

"I... I... school has begun, *didi*," stuttered Tenzin.

School had begun, but Rhea knew she was too ashamed to reveal that her father was not letting her visit the village after Rhea had spoken rudely to him during his previous visit.

They watched the minister mount the platform at the village square and make his usual promises of providing them water, electricity, a bridge, and security from the miscreants. Someone from the crowd directed his attention towards the field. The minister and his henchmen walked towards the trench and inspected it as one villager animatedly explained the system to them. He also directed their attention towards the hills on the border, where they squinted to see a batch of villagers laying the pipeline and seeing the minister dumbfounded, exhilarated Rhea. The villagers then proudly pointed towards her.

He walked towards Rhea, Sania, and Tenzin just as Saahil made their way towards them.

"It's a nice little project there you have going on," he said, stressing the word *little* without a smile.

"Thank you, Ministerji," said Rhea with a grin. I took your advice about doing something for the villagers seriously, so you are the true inspiration behind it."

The sarcasm was hard to miss, and the minister obviously knew she was mocking him. But he restrained himself in the presence of the villagers. He didn't want to ruin his impression in front of them just before the elections since they obviously adored her.

"That is very thoughtful of you. I wish you all the best

of luck," he said, still without a smile.

He then grabbed Tenzin's hand and walked away.

#

Upon arriving at Tashkar the following day, Rhea and Sania were met with an unexpected sight. Instead of the children, they saw several villagers seated on the cold, hard ground, looking sad and gloomy. Some were even crying aloud. Initially, Rhea feared that something had happened to the village headman, but her worries were put to rest when she saw him seated on a cot on the platform amongst the villagers at the village square.

When they saw Rhea, the villagers rose together, and one of them ran towards her.

"What happened?" asked Rhea.

"Last night, somebody destroyed all the pipes that we had laid in the mountains, and even the trench beside the field has been tampered with," said the villager. "One month of all our hard work has been wrecked."

Rhea was dazed, and before he could continue, she darted towards the hill. She didn't know what had overcome her, but she kept running without paying heed to Sania, who was imploring her to stop. The villagers, too, began sprinting after her. She ran up the mountain at breakneck speed and saw evidence of the devastation all along the way. She didn't know for how long she had been running, but at some point, exhaustion took over, and she could not proceed further, causing her to collapse to the ground in a heap, gasping for breath. What she witnessed broke her heart. Along the mountain slope, pipes were broken and strewn everywhere. The rocks and cement stubs that held them had been wrecked, too. All the villagers' hard work lay tattered on the ground, like someone had torn a piece of paper and tossed the bits around.

181

"It's those same Pakistani and Chinese vandals who trouble us throughout the year. They want to make our lives miserable. They even destroyed the meshwork of branches that we had created next to the field," said a villager.

Rhea was filled with rage, like a volcano erupting, since she knew that the vandalism was not done by anyone from the outside. It was the minister's way of getting back at her for standing up to him and helping the villagers. He couldn't accept that the village had become self-sufficient and less dependent on him. He couldn't let a tourist do in a month what he had not done for them in years.

As they slowly walked down the mountain together, they took time to process the enormity of the destruction they had just witnessed. Rhea was lost in thought, silently contemplating her next move. Despite the devastation, she wanted to remain resolute and determined not to give up. She was someone who never shied away from a challenge. However, she could not help but feel deeply saddened by what had happened. She also couldn't help but feel sorry for the villagers who had worked so hard to build the ice stupa. When they finally reached the village, they saw that the minister and his group had arrived, looking equally distraught.

"I heard what happened to your project and came at once," he told the villagers, keeping one eye on Rhea. "That is why it is paramount to catch these vandals as soon as possible. I will help you, so don't lose hope."

Rhea had been holding back for a long time, but something inside her finally snapped. The minister's taunts, the hard work put in by her friends, and the disappointment on the faces of the villagers all piled up like dry leaves waiting to catch fire. She was not one to be intimidated, especially when she was a victim of injustice. She knew the minister was manipulating the villagers' emotions and couldn't tolerate it any longer.

"You are the one responsible for this!" she screamed from her place.

Everyone turned to her in surprise. She could see the minister's face contort with rage for a moment and then recover immediately. Never in his wildest dreams did he think that someone in Tashkar would openly accuse him of any wrongdoing.

"Excuse me?" he asked calmly.

"Why don't you admit that you sent those people to destroy our *ice stupa*?" asked Rhea.

"Are you out of your mind?" he asked without raising his voice, smiling and mocking Rhea. "How can you make an accusation like that? And why would I do such a thing?"

"Because you want this village to rot in poverty and be your slaves forever," screamed Rhea.

The minister laughed at Rhea like she was a madwoman who made no sense.

"I have been working for these people all my life. What will a tourist like you know about true service? Don't make such a big deal about your part-time project," said the minister.

The term *part-time* project only incensed Rhea further.

"So you admit to having jeopardized it," said Rhea. "And in what way have you helped the people of Tashkar? These people have been rotting in poverty for ages. You have not provided them anything in return for their loyalty. You want them to be your slaves forever."

The minister finally gave up putting up a façade of nonchalance.

"You come here and make such allegations about a public servant like me, who has given his life in service to these people. I am being nice to you, yet to accuse me of things I haven't done. I will put you in place," he said, stomping off before Rhea could say anything more.

Rhea stood her ground, seething as Sania held her by her shoulders, trying to calm her down.

Chapter Twenty

"*Didi,* let's take a break from all this and go sightseeing," Sania said to Rhea, who had been sitting irate all morning along with the children, who seemed baffled by everything happening in their village. She could not take any classes after witnessing the massacre of her *ice stupa* project and the arrogance of the minister. The villagers were back to ploughing their fields, their morale being destroyed after seeing what had become of all the hard work they had put in over the last month. But unlike Rhea, they were used to these disappointments, and life went on for them. If they didn't get back to their fields, they wouldn't survive. It was as simple as that.

"I am in no mood to go sightseeing, Sania," said Rhea. "How can I enjoy anything right now after what we've been through."

"That's exactly why I want you to go out, *didi,*" said Sania. "You haven't been out of Tashkar in over four months."

It was true. After the sightseeing they had done in the initial two weeks of her trip, Rhea had dedicated herself to Tashkar, and amidst all the activities there, she had not realized how time had flown by.

"It'll help you clear your mind," offered Sania.

Rhea thought about it and felt claustrophobic. Suddenly, the thought of leaving the village for a while and becoming a tourist again seemed very appealing to her. It also made her realize how frustrating it must be for the villagers to have their hopes repeatedly dashed for so many years. She was a tourist who had had her first significant setback here, and that itself had drained the life out of her. It was no wonder the headman had turned so pessimistic after everything he had witnessed in the village.

"So where do you want to go?" asked Rhea.

"Magnetic hill?" Sania asked, looking at Saahil, sitting on the platform quietly listening to the conversation.

"Good idea," he said, and Rhea noticed him grin mischievously at Sania.

They waded across the river, got into Saahil's minivan, and drove away. It had been a long time since she had been on a drive in Leh besides getting to Tashkar every day, and she admired the landscape as if she had just arrived. The chilly breeze stung her face as she peered out of the window from the backseat, and it refreshed her. The majestic Indus River flowed languidly by the side of the road. The dark brown mountains with white snow-capped peaks stood imposingly by the sides, far away, as if keeping a watch on them all the time. They drove for an hour to what she assumed was the outskirts of Leh. Suddenly, Saahil stopped the car in the middle of the road.

"We are here," he said with the same mischievous grin he had given Sania earlier.

Rhea looked around. Theirs was the only vehicle on that stretch of the highway with mountain peaks in the distance. On either side of the road was a barren rock-strewn land. The road ahead was uphill and so straight that she felt it would continue to infinity. It was no different to any other highway she had seen in various parts of Leh.

"Is this some kind of joke you both are playing on me?" Rhea asked, raising her eyebrow.

Both Saahil and Sania laughed. Saahil pointed to a yellow board by the side of the road with **Magnetic Hill** written on it. *The phenomenon that defies gravity. Park your vehicle in the box marked with paint on the road and experience the wonder* it said.

Once she read the board, Saahil parked the car at the designated spot and shifted the car into neutral. At first, nothing happened.

"Wow, this is amazing. Who knew parking the car in the middle of nowhere was so much fun?" Rhea said sarcastically.

"Wait for a few minutes, *didi*," giggled Sania.

Within a minute or so, the car began moving forward. It was slow at first, but it picked up slowly. Rhea looked ahead at the road, and it was impossible that they were moving forward with the engine turned off since it was uphill. She looked at the speedometer, which said 20 km/hr.

"This is impossible!" exclaimed Rhea. "How can this be happening?"

"It's called the *Magnetic Hill*," said Saahil straight-faced. "The magnetic pull of the mountain is so strong that it can pull cars towards it."

She looked at the mountain he was pointing at in the distance. *A hill that can pull metals as huge as a car towards it.* It sounded ridiculous.

"The magnetic force is so strong that the airplanes have to fly at a higher altitude here than normal for fear of being sucked in," he said gravely.

Rhea looked from his poker face to that of Sania, who was stifling a laugh. This was too far-fetched a story for Rhea to believe.

"Tell me the truth," she said, pinching Sania's arm.

Sania screamed in pain and then giggled.

"It's just a myth *didi*," she said. "In reality, this is an optical illusion because of the layout of the hills. They obstruct the view of the horizon. So, in reality, this road is actually downhill, but the illusion is that of a car moving uphill by itself."

Rhea looked back at the road, the mountains in the distance, and the horizon. It was true that the horizon was obscured, but even after Sania told her that the road was not uphill, it was hard for her to believe it since it didn't seem so. But at least that explanation made more sense than the Magnetic Hill theory that Saahil was trying to pull off.

Rhea saw Saahil smiling faintly to himself.

"Who knew you had a sense of humour," she said, and all three laughed.

"I want to record this on my phone," Rhea said, pulling out her smartphone. They exited the car, and Rhea pointed the camera at Sania. Sania introduced the place like a tour guide. She then pointed at the billboard with the instructions. Rhea panned the camera from her to the board and then to the road, which gave the illusion of being uphill. They got into the car with Sania narrating the cock and bull story of magnetism that Saahil had just narrated to them. Rhea recorded as the vehicle moved magically forward in neutral. They exited the car, and Sania explained the real reason for the phenomenon.

"You have a natural flair for this," Rhea told her.

"Thank you, *didi*," Sania said shyly, twirling the edges of her hijab.

"I will record all the places in Leh with you as the

guide so that once I go back home, I can watch them repeatedly and remember both Leh and you," said Rhea.

Tears streamed down Sania's cheeks instantly at the thought of Rhea leaving, and she embraced her warmly. Rhea was not much for overt displays of affection, but she, too, couldn't help but embrace her for a long time.

"Come now, don't make me cry," said Rhea as she pulled apart. "Where else are you going to take me now?"

Afterward, they went to the stunning Shey Palace on Shey Mountain. Rhea was captivated by the grandeur of the three-storey palace, complete with a gold-topped victory Stupa. She recorded Sania as she described the palace, including its two-storey statue of Shakyamuni Buddha made of copper and gold and the beautiful frescoes adorning the walls. They could see the entire city of Shey spread out from the palace.

"Shey means a mirror, and it is said that the town of Shey is a reflection of the palace," said Sania to the camera.

"Wow, that was wonderful," said Rhea, turning off the camera.

By then, it was late, and Rhea had thoroughly enjoyed her day. The places they visited and Saahil's and Sania's company had made her momentarily forget about the disappointment of the ice stupa project being wrecked. It made her realize the value of having good friends beside her in times of need. Until then, she never believed in sharing her thoughts with her friends. She felt it was unnecessary since one had to deal with one's life without giving someone else control over it. But now she realized that friends make a difference, especially if they are like Sania and Saahil.

Now that her mind was clear, a renewed vigour had replaced the disappointment of earlier that morning.

"So what do we do next, *didi*?" asked Sania on the drive home.

"Tomorrow is a new day," said Rhea with a smile. "So we start afresh."

#

Rhea asked all the villagers to assemble at the village square the next day. The morale of the people seated there was low, and a sense of defeat, which they were so accustomed to, was writ large over their faces.

"I can see that all of you are disappointed," said Rhea, scanning each of their faces as she spoke from the platform. "And I don't blame you."

The words seem to deflate them even more. She saw a woman silently shed a tear. Rhea walked down from the platform towards the woman, who stood up immediately and held her hand.

"I don't blame you because I was disappointed and upset. And this is my first time. You have had to face similar disappointments for years."

The woman buried her face in Rhea's hands. She saw a couple of heads nod and turn their gaze to the floor.

"But now the time has come for these disappointments to end," said Rhea, addressing everyone. "So what if some miscreants have destroyed our hard work? We will work twice as hard, show twice the determination, and tell them they must work twice as hard to push us down. We lose the day we stop trying, so we will not stop."

Suddenly, all of them seemed to listen to her with rapt attention.

"Do you want to stop and give up?" Rhea asked the woman, who was still clutching her hand.

"We will not stop," said the woman tearfully.

"We will never stop!" shouted a villager in the crowd, and suddenly, they all screamed in unison with a renewed resolve instilled in them.

"Fate has been unkind to you all. Let's work so hard that even fate gives up, and let's win," said Rhea.

The villagers stood up and gave a cry of victory.

"Wow, that was such a hair-raising speech, *didi*," said Sania. "I have goosebumps all over."

"Time for talk is over, Sania," said Rhea, "Let's get to work now."

#

And everyone got to work in all earnest. All the villagers worked on the ice stupa this time as if their life depended on it. She saw men, women, and children, irrespective of age, carrying bricks on their shoulders up the treacherous mountains throughout the morning. They had no modern equipment and relied on manual labour only. A group of villagers began chopping wood from the forest's trees and hauled them down the mountain to the trench beside the fields where the stupa would be set up. There were a few people designated to only carry drinking water and meals to the ones at work so that the chain of continuity wasn't broken. Many suffered minor cuts and burns while working, and Rhea tended to all of them at the clinic. One man suffered a snake bite and succumbed despite Rhea's best efforts since he could not get the anti-snake venom on time because of its scarcity in Leh. Throughout their work, they kept hearing shelling at the border, during which they would all drop flat on the ground, but thankfully, no stray bullet came their way. Rhea even spotted the headman at the trench a few times, silently supervising the work and giving the villagers suggestions when he thought Rhea was not watching him.

So, what they achieved in more than a month on their first attempt was completed in 20 days in their second stint. Even Rhea couldn't believe that they had finished the job so fast. She called up Divya and Sardarji, who arrived within a week.

"Completing the work in just one and half months is so impressive," said Divya, who had just inspected the entire pipeline from the hills up to the trench with Rhea, Saahil, and *Sardarji*.

"You'll be even more impressed when I tell you the challenges the people faced along the way," said Rhea.

She then explained how the project was wrecked when they were halfway through and had to restart everything.

"Unbelievable," *Sardarji* said once Rhea had narrated the events of the last one and a half months.

"Yes, it's incredible," agreed Divya. But the result of all this hard work will only be known tonight," she added.

All of them nodded in unison. The fruit of their labour depended on whether the water would flow through the pipes with enough force and form an *ice stupa*.

#

On that freezing night, the entire village gathered around the trench. All eyes were fixed at the centre, where a single pipe had been erected almost 20 feet high above the ground. The pipe's nozzle was directed upwards. Around it, leafless tree branches had been cut and heaped to form a framework for the ice to form, creating an enormous mesh.

Rhea shivered in her warm clothes. She was covered in so many layers of clothing that she was hardly seen.

"I don't know what you used to do on those nights in this cold with your husband during the honeymoon," she whispered to Divya more out of nervousness, trying to humour and calm herself.

"You must be really nervous," said Divya. "You never joke about these things otherwise."

Rhea was nervous, but there was a reason for it. In the last one and a half months, she had given the villagers a purpose towards which they had worked day and night. That purpose had now turned into hope, and she could see the same nervous anticipation on each of their faces. If it didn't work, she didn't know how she could face them anymore. After all the disappointments they had dealt with in life, she was not prepared to see them let down again because of her. She had put all her hopes on it and would feel like she failed them if it didn't work.

"Let us begin!" screamed *Sardarji* excitedly, pointing his camera at the centre of the trench. He, too, couldn't wait to get the contraption working.

A single flare was launched into the night sky from the trench to signal the person on the mountain to open the pipe valve. The flare surged high and burst into a yellow flame, lighting up the dark night sky. Everyone waited eagerly at the trench; nothing happened for the first five minutes.

"Do you think there is a leak somewhere along the way?" asked Rhea, hugging herself in anticipation.

"I don't think so since we checked the pipeline thoroughly. It takes a few minutes for the pressure to build up," said Sardarji.

Just as he said the words, a spurt of water emerged from the pipe high in the air, almost to a height of 30 feet, and descended back to the ground. Everyone watched with bated breath as the pressure slowly increased over time.

"Look, the water is freezing, *didi*," screamed Sania

excitedly.

Everyone looked towards Sania's point and gasped. As she said, tiny icicles were forming over the meshwork of branches.

"That is amazing," said *Sardarji*, holding up his camera in admiration.

The entire village burst out into screams of victory. Divya and Rhea hugged in delight while *Sardarji* broke into impromptu *bhangra*. It was just the beginning of the formation of the icicles, and the eventual ice stupa would take months to form, but still, Rhea knew it was the beginning of the solution to the village's water problems.

Rhea took Sania and Saahil in an embrace. Sania let out tears of joy while Saahil stared at the spurting water proudly.

In the corner, away from everyone, the headman stood all alone, looking at the ground. When he looked up, Rhea saw tears in his eyes.

Chapter Twenty-One

Over several weeks, the ice stupa gradually grew larger, just as the hopes and spirits of the villagers had been uplifted. Each night, when the temperatures dropped significantly, the water was released from the pipe and would then freeze around the mesh of branches. During the day, the water supply was shut off as the weather was warmer, which did not allow the flowing water to freeze immediately. Tiny ice crystals began to form on the branches daily, and the artificial glacier slowly hardened over weeks. The objective was for the glacier to remain solid during the winter and then melt during the summer, providing water when the river dried up.

Sardarji was the first to leave for home after witnessing the creation of the ice stupa, and he seemed the most excited among the group. On the other hand, Divya stayed back for three more days to do some sightseeing with Rhea and Sania. During this time, Divya captured a video of Sania explaining the mechanism of the ice stupa so that she could show it to her colleagues in the office and let them know about her experience. Finally, Divya left for her home in Bangalore, and the village of Tashkar returned to its routine.

But what happened next in the village was something nobody anticipated. A few weeks after Divya's departure, a group of journalists appeared in Tashkar, and their camerapersons began recording in front of the ice stupa. The villagers, who had never seen a video camera until then, were baffled by what they were seeing, but they answered all the questions put to them by the journalists. Once the villagers informed the journalists about how Rhea had been instrumental in setting up the *ice stupa*, they requested them to bring Rhea to them, which they hurriedly did.

"What is happening?" asked a surprised Rhea, who was greeted by a barrage of flashing cameras when she arrived at the village that morning.

"An architect uploaded a video of the ice stupa, which caught the eye of a news channel and then went viral. We are here to cover the project," informed one journalist.

Rhea recollected the video that Divya had captured. She assumed that Divya had uploaded it to some social media platform. Rhea was both surprised and happy at the same time. When asked about the project, she explained in detail how the plan was conceived, their difficulties while executing it, and how the villagers had toiled day and night to make it a reality. Furthermore, she informed them about the significant contribution made by Divya and Sardarji in constructing the ice stupa. Rhea also took the opportunity to explain the villagers' plight - the lack of electricity, the unavailability of a bridge to access the village, and the absence of voter IDs.

The interview shed light on the dire situation of the village of Tashkar, which garnered unprecedented attention on social media and news channels. Several news anchors reported on the village's condition, leading to an outpouring of funds and support for the villagers. An NGO stepped in to fund the construction of a bridge to access the village, which was approved immediately. The government faced backlash for not doing enough for the village and announced measures to register the land in the name of the villagers and enrol them as voters. The local elections were postponed until the villagers received their voter ID's. Electricity, which had always been a mere election promise, became a demand from people outside Tashkar for the villagers. These changes marked a turning point for the village, finally bringing hope for a better future.

#

Rhea was at the clinic in Tashkar, discussing health issues with a few of the village's womenfolk, when she spotted the familiar cavalcade of the minister, Bhadrapala Tsering, approaching the village. The minister looked angry, and Rhea understood why. He had lost all his fake votes from Tashkar, and the media's attention had highlighted the poor state of the village, further tarnishing his reputation. The villagers had also lost their respect for him after realizing he had failed to fulfil his promises for years, while Rhea managed to help them out in just a few months.

As she waited, she anticipated he would walk directly toward her and confront her, but instead, he trudged to the village square. Once there, he climbed up the platform and instructed his assistants to gather all the villagers who had not assembled as they would have. The villagers made their way to the square one by one, unwillingly. The headman took his customary position beside him and seemed as disinterested as always.

"What does he want today? He has no promises left to make, and there is nothing he can do for Tashkar right now," said Saahil.

It was true. It was the minister's first visit after the social media attention that Tashkar had received. Until now, he had made a conscious effort to stay away when the media was present since he was at the receiving end of the brickbats from every news channel.

"He has come to take the credit for the construction of the bridge," suggested Rhea, rolling her eyes.

The foundation for the bridge was laid a week ago with the help of the NGO that offered to cover the construction costs. The villagers wanted Rhea to lay the foundation stone, as they believed she was responsible for the positive changes in the village. However, Rhea declined the offer and requested the headman perform the honours instead.

The minister looked at all the villagers and then at Rhea out of the corner of his eye to make sure she was watching him.

"My dear friends of Tashkar," he began. "For years, I have been struggling to improve your lives, and I am happy that things are finally taking a turn for the better for you all."

There was a murmur amongst the villagers. Saahil spat on the ground disgustedly, as usual.

"I have spoken to the authorities and instructed them to complete the work on the bridge as soon as possible," he said.

"Unbelievable," said Saahil, looking at Rhea stupefied. "You were right. He is taking credit for the bridge."

"And now that the bridge work has begun, work on erecting the electricity poles will also soon commence under my guidance," he declared.

"What took you so long?" demanded someone in the crowd.

"Rhea, madam, did in eight months what you haven't been able to do in the last ten years," said another villager.

One of the minister's bodyguards, dressed in a grey safari suit, advanced in anger, scanning the crowd for the person who had dared to speak to the minister so brazenly. However, before the bodyguard could take any action, the minister silently extended his hand and pulled him back without wiping the smile off his face.

"So you believe that your beloved tourist is responsible for all this?" he asked the audience with a smile.

His question was met with nods of affirmation from the crowd.

"And you think that your tourist madam is a noble soul doing all this to improve your lives because she is the most selfless person on earth?" he asked again, grinning.

Everyone nodded again. Someone began shouting Rhea's name, and they all started chanting it together. Rhea was touched by the love and affection they were showering on her. The minister patiently waited for the chants to subside.

"Ever since I saw your tourist madam here, I wondered who she was," said the minister. "I mean, who is this woman really?" he asked, pointing at Rhea.

They all looked at her.

"I wondered why a doctor, no less a surgeon with so many fancy degrees, from a city like Mumbai has left behind a life of wealth and thriving medical practice and come here to serve the people, a place where no doctors ever want to come," he said, pointing at the villagers.

He inhaled deeply to let whatever he was saying sink in. His confident, arrogant manner suddenly bothered Rhea. There was something sinister about it all.

"And once our little village of Tashkar became famous, its name splashed around in the newspapers and TV channels, this tourist madam shot to fame, and those news outlets went gaga over her," he declared. "And that's when a headline in one newspaper in Mumbai caught my eye when I was there last week."

Suddenly, Rhea felt her pulse quicken as a suppressed

memory slowly surfaced. She prayed that the minister would not mention the one thing she feared most.

"And that headline was - KILLER DOCTOR TRANSFORMS A VILLAGE," he said dramatically, stretching his arms and showing the newspaper article to everyone even though none of them in the crowd could read.

There was a buzz in the crowd, and Rhea was afraid to look at them. Her eyes were firmly on the minister and his on hers.

"And when I dug deeper, I found that this tourist madam of yours was caught for fraud, for operating on a dead patient for the sake of money, and she was dismissed from her job, and her license to practice was cancelled," he said emphatically.

Rhea's heart sank, and the colour from her face drained completely.

"What rubbish is he speaking," said an otherwise demure Sania angrily. "How can he make such false allegations?"

But Saahil stood silently, scrutinizing Rhea's face as if he knew what the minister said was true. The villagers began whispering to one another frantically, unable to digest this new information.

"It all makes sense now," said the minister. "This woman is no ordinary tourist. She came here not intending to help you all. She came here with a mission to help herself. She wanted to be in the spotlight by saying that she had done something good so that she could prove to the people back home that she was a good person so that she could be reinstated at her hospital and get back to her work of fleecing innocent patients," declared the minister.

Rhea knew that this part of his statement was not true,

but she didn't have the strength to deny it. She never wanted to be in the spotlight—there would never have been a spotlight if not for Divya—but she maintained a stoic silence.

"So don't be fooled by this woman," said the minister. "You are all just a project like the ice stupa for her. She will soon go away to her well-paying job in her well-to-do city, and you will all be left to fend for yourself. And when that happens, the only person who can help you is me," he declared.

After making the impact he wanted, the minister folded his hands, grinned at the people, and walked away.

#

Rhea stood in silence while the villagers glared at her accusingly, their faces contorted with hatred solely directed towards her.

"Traitor!" screamed the headman, his face twitching with anger.

She couldn't look him in the eye. She remembered how she had questioned his morality when he had done nothing about the minister distributing handouts to the villagers in return for their fake votes. The allegations against her were far worse than the ones she had levelled against him back then. She found it difficult to look the villagers in the eye. She felt she had let them down, even though she hadn't. The minister's accusations about her actions in Mumbai were accurate, but his claims about her supposed wrongdoing in Tashkar were completely baseless. She had acted with pure intentions, and there was no hidden motive behind her actions.

"Grab her and tie her to the tree. We will show her how we deal with traitors," commanded the headman.

Rhea was taken aback by the man's harsh tone and sudden resentment toward her. However, before she could dwell on the thought, she was seized by both arms and pulled roughly towards a nearby tree. She struggled to break free from the firm grip but to no avail. No one came to her aid, and even though Sania was crying out, two strong men were holding her back while Saahil was nowhere to be seen.

Before she knew it, they bound her to the tree with a rope around her torso. They bound together her hands and feet so tight that the fibres of the rope cut through her skin. *What kind of madness is this? Why was she being punished in Tashkar for something she had done in Mumbai?*

Just then, the minister appeared before Rhea, grinning from ear to ear. It was as if he had succeeded in his mission. To see his nemesis strapped helplessly to a tree in pain, with all the villagers turning against her, seemed an apt revenge for what she had put him through in the past few months with her insolence and insubordination.

"So now you know what happens to people who try to undermine my authority," the minister said, bringing his face close to Rhea.

"I have done nothing wrong in this village," replied Rhea defiantly.

"Until now," said the minister. "But I am sure you were just waiting for the right time to cheat these people just like you cheated your patients back home."

It was a vile remark. Again, Rhea couldn't answer his accusation for some reason. *Why did she feel ashamed whenever he mentioned what she had done at White Arc?* When she was at home after being fired from her job, she always justified herself by saying that she had done nothing wrong. Whenever she spoke to her father, she defended herself, saying she had done nothing that others in her place wouldn't have done. Then why could she not do the same in front of the villagers?

"And I won't let you cheat these people, either," the minister said with a grin.

And saying so, to Rhea's horror, he pulled out a gun and pointed it at her. *What was it with these people and guns?* And where was Saahil when she needed him the most?

The minister held the gun firmly pointed at her. *Surely, it must be empty.* He had to be bluffing. There was no way he could shoot her. There was no way the villagers would let her be shot in broad daylight. After all, she had been with them for the last eight months. But to her surprise, nobody moved.

The minister pulled the trigger. She heard the click of the hammer, and the next minute, she heard a bang echo across the silent village. A sudden shooting pain drew her attention to her belly, where warm blood was oozing into her palms. *He shot me!* She would have collapsed if she wasn't tied to the tree. It was all over. She was going to die in an alien land, amidst the snow-capped mountains, away from her parents. *How would her father react to the news of her death? Who would her mother annoy regarding proposals? Will her brother post her obituary on Facebook?*

"Are you okay?" she heard Saahil's voice beside her.

Where was he when she needed him? What was the point of coming after she had been shot?

"Don't worry, I will get the bullet out. I am the best doctor in town," he said.

Rhea was confused. What was he talking about? Had he lost his senses like every other person in the village? She looked up and was stunned to see the face staring back at her was not Saahil's but of her patient who died in White Arc. *What in the world was happening?*

"Don't worry. It's all going to be fine," he said with a smile.

Something reassuring about the way he said it instantly comforted her. The pain seemed to have subsided, and she felt positively numb. *What kind of magic was this?*

She looked at his face. It was almost Angelic. *Was she dead already and in heaven?* But the very next minute, everything changed as his face contorted. A sinister grin replaced the comforting smile. Blood oozed from the corner of his mouth. Blood spurted from his abdomen as well, just like her. And in his right hand, he was holding a knife.

"What are you doing?" asked Rhea, terrified.

"I have to get the bullet out, don't I?" he asked. "And how can I do it without cutting you open?"

The world has gone crazy around me. None of this made sense. Or was it she who had lost her mind? That could be possible since she had been through a rollercoaster of emotions in the past eight months. It must have all been too much for her mind to take at some point, and it had broken down.

As the knife drew closer to her stomach, Rhea began screaming for help. Nobody moved a muscle to help her. It was as if they were all watching a movie plot unfold. She continued to cry as the knife plunged into her belly and twisted viciously.

Chapter Twenty-Two

Rhea woke up gasping for breath as if she had just surfaced after nearly drowning. The first thing she noticed was that she was not tied to any tree in Tashkar but was lying on her bed, the sheets she was clutching so tight that her knuckles turned white. It took her a few more moments to realize that she was in her hotel room in Leh and not being executed in public. She was completely drenched in sweat, even though the room was freezing cold. She had just been through another nightmare. *Was I screaming in my sleep?* She waited a while to see if anyone would come and check on her if she had actually been screaming, but thankfully, no one came.

She sat up on the bed and hugged her knees to her chest. The morning rays filtered through the grills of the window, casting a black pattern on her bed. *Do you still call it a nightmare if you have it in the morning?* She would have chuckled at the thought any other day, but not that day. It had been a while since she had had a nightmare. It began after she was fired from her job at White Arc, but she hadn't had one since she had been in Tashkar. But every nightmare seemed as real and frightening as the previous one. For someone who was never afraid of anything in the real world, she found it embarrassing to be frightened by a bad dream, but it was something that was not under her control.

How could she face the people of Tashkar now? It had been a week since the minister had revealed her past to the villagers. And the week had been tougher than the one in Mumbai after she had suffered the trial by the media. She didn't have the resolve to appear in front of anyone in Tashkar. What was worse was that she found it difficult to meet Sania since Sania had always considered Rhea her idol. *What kind of idol had she turned into?* Over the past week, she had remained locked in her hotel room and instructed the old man at the reception counter not to let anyone in, not even Sania. She stayed inside all day as if the world outside had turned apocalyptic. She had not even called her parents, especially her father, who was her closest confidante. It was the first time she had ever shied away from the world, and she could not understand why since she was never the one to be bothered by other's opinions.

There was a knock on the door. She walked to it, and the hotel proprietor stood stooping with a smile.

"Your lady friend is here to see you. She has been coming every morning and evening to meet you," he said.

By now, the proprietor knew Sania well since she had been there so often since Rhea had landed in Leh. He struggled to understand why Rhea was not letting her best friend in.

"Please tell her I don't want to meet anyone," Rhea said politely and shut the door.

#

Rhea remained indoors for three more weeks. For the second time in her life, she did nothing useful during that time, just like in Mumbai after she faced the trial by the media. She would wake up in the morning, freshen up, and stay indoors, doing nothing but dwelling on the past. The proprietor looked after her meals, which he brought to her room. Every day, the same thoughts lingered in her mind.

The question that kept nagging her was whether she had acted incorrectly back home at White Arc. And if she was wrong, how could she have been oblivious to it? What happened to that optimistic medical student determined to impact the world positively? Had she lost herself in her quest to reach the top? Now, she had transformed into a confident and assertive consultant with an air of entitlement. As a medical student, money had never motivated her while visiting people's homes. But now, how had her decisions in life changed? Why was she deciding whether to operate on a patient based on their financial status? Didn't everyone deserve equal treatment? After all, she had treated everyone for free at the Tashkar clinic for almost a year. So why had she chosen to operate only on well-off patients at White Arc?

The question that was nagging her even more was why she had been operating on patients who didn't require surgery. The young boy whom she falsely diagnosed to have appendicitis. It was not by accident but on purpose. How could she have cut him open when there was nothing wrong with him? Of course, she was competent enough to see that the surgery would go perfectly fine, but how had she justified doing it? To make it worse, he had lost an academic year for no reason other than that Rhea had to make up the numbers for the hospital to please the MD and get ahead of her colleagues.

And then came the patient who had a fall from the building. Didn't she decide to operate on him because the employer told her that money was not an issue? Would she have attempted the surgery if he had not made that assurance? And wasn't she aware that he was dead before she began the surgery? Had her soul been so corrupted by the demands of her employers and colleagues that she had given up on all her ethics? How could she justify doing such a thing?

And yet she had justified everything, saying she had done nothing wrong. Every time they pointed a finger at her, she deflected the accusations, saying that she had done nothing that others in her place would not have done. And what was worse was that she never felt sorry about it. But the day the minister revealed her past in front of the villagers who had accepted and trusted her, with whom she had spent almost a year, she realized she was wrong. All those promises she made as a student came rushing back to her when she looked into the eyes of those simple, unquestioning villagers. The way Sania looked up to her, the way Saahil respected her, and the way Shainaz was proud of her made her realize what an impact she had made in everyone's lives, and that impact had only amplified the gravity of the mistakes in her past. The system had corrupted her. She had the power to oppose it all, yet she had chosen to become a part of it.

Rhea thought long and hard and finally came to a decision. She looked out of her hotel room window and saw that the sky had turned a collusion of red & yellow with the setting sun. She would have to leave this place and return home. She could not face the people of Tashkar at any cost. It was too painful to be amidst people who trusted her. Suddenly, her home, with all the viciously attacking people who were baying for her blood, seemed more inviting. She would return to the wolves and decide her next action.

But before that, she had to have one last look at Tashkar.

#

Rhea used her keys to unlock the clinic, making sure not to draw too much attention to herself. She then headed straight to the examination room without turning on the oil lamp. The sun had set, leaving a dark, black sky filled with grey clouds that matched Rhea's sombre mood. She had managed to make her way to Tashkar and the clinic without being seen by many villagers. The ones who did, looked at her in confusion as if trying to figure out where she had disappeared over the last one month.

Rhea was sitting in a chair in the dark, gazing out the window, taking in the atmosphere of the life she had embraced over the past year. She reminisced about the first time she visited Tashkar when Sania took her there to showcase the excellent work Saahil was doing in the village. That one visit set off a series of events culminating in her current state of sitting in the chair and reflecting on a beautiful year.

She initially wanted to escape from her village, but her inquisitive nature and determination to face challenges made her remain in Tashkar. As a result, the foreign land ended up embracing her. Reflecting on the past year's events, she was amazed at how her life had undergone such a remarkable transformation. After she lost her license to practice, she expected the year to be the worst of her life, but instead, she found herself doing things she never thought possible.

Never in her wildest dreams did she think she would teach biology to a group of children one day. To think that a woman who gave lectures at international surgery conferences in front of big names in the healthcare sector would one day be teaching children of a village about plants and human beings was unfathomable to her. And she had enjoyed every minute of it.

She had then gone on to open a clinic where she treated patients free of cost. She treated every ailment, sometimes even using her phone to access medical books since she had lost touch with the subjects besides surgery. And it felt liberating since she didn't have to fall prey to the pressures of her bosses wanting her to see more patients to fill the hospital coffers or her colleagues who tried to thwart her progress so that she would not supersede them.

If that was incredible, what she did next was simply out of this world. She built an ice stupa, something she had never heard of before coming to Leh. When she first heard about it from Divya on the Zanskar Trek, she didn't pay much attention. However, when she wanted to help the villagers solve their water problems and get back at the challenge thrown by the minister, she gave it serious thought. With the help of her friends, she pulled it off in grand style despite the challenging circumstances. This set in motion a chain of events that led to the village expecting electricity soon, a bridge that had been promised for years, and the land they could now call their own.

During her stay in Leh, Rhea not only helped the village of Tashkar but also benefited greatly from her experience there. She had arrived in Leh after a major controversy had turned her life upside down. Rhea was brash and arrogant then and would do anything to achieve her goals. However, meeting Sania and her family had a profound impact on her. Their cheerful and determined attitudes, despite their hardships, inspired Rhea to change her approach towards achieving her goals. Along the way, she made some real friends for the first time, like the hardworking Divya and the seemingly boisterous but kind-hearted Sardarji. All of them taught Rhea valuable lessons about the importance of resilience, determination, and the actual value of friendship.

After spending time with the villagers of Tashkar, she realized that being number one wasn't the only thing that mattered. Making a difference in someone else's life was equally important. The struggles faced by the villagers reminded her of the promises she had made to herself as a student, and being there gave her a chance to fulfil them.

But what an adventure it had been as well! From gun-toting citizens to beedi-toting *dais*, she had witnessed scenes she never imagined herself to see. Completing the Zanskar trek even though she ended with a fall, Saahil getting shot in the leg, shelling at the border, vandalism of the village and her ice stupa, and a minister distributing cash for votes, it had all been the stuff of movies back when she was in the comfort of her living room at home. And everything had made an everlasting impact on her.

At that moment, for the first time in a year, Rhea missed her parents and her father. She missed talking to him, taking his advice, and receiving his unconditional support.

She pulled out her phone and dialled his number with the urgency of needing life support.

"Hello, *beta*," she heard his voice on the second ring.

"Hi, Dad," Rhea said.

"What happened, *beta*?" asked her father.

He was on the phone hundreds of miles away, yet he knew something was wrong by just listening to her voice.

"I want to tell you something, Dad," she whispered.

"Yes?" he asked gently.

Rhea inhaled deeply. She prepared herself for the immense disappointment that she would cause him. After all those years of unconditional support, she would throw it all away.

"Dad, whatever I was accused of in White Arc was true," she said.

Sitting there, she braced herself for the words she didn't want to hear. She knew what was coming. He would express his disappointment in her, reminding her of the values he had instilled in her. She knew he would say that her behaviour had disgraced the whole family. He would have to hang his head in shame forever.

"I always knew it was true," he said.

That was the last thing she had expected him to say.

"How?" was the only word Rhea could utter.

"Because you are my child. You don't need to say things for me to understand," he said.

"Then why didn't you say anything?" she asked.

"Because I wanted you to realize your mistake on your own. I have raised you to be a good person, and I knew that you would come to me one day and tell me that you had committed a mistake, which you have now. Everyone makes mistakes at some point in their life. It's what you do after the mistake; how that mistake changes you is what matters. And because no matter how many mistakes you make, you are still my child, and I will always love you," he said in his calm, caring voice.

Rhea was already brimming with many thoughts. Hearing his words, she was overwhelmed with emotion. Her father was her superhero. She wanted to tell him many things then, but words failed her.

"I love you too, Dad," she said and broke down.

#

"Come with me," said Saahil, startling Rhea, who had been seated alone in the clinic after speaking to her father.

Their conversation lasted over an hour, during which Rhea spoke her heart out. Her eyes revealed she had been crying, and even though Saahil had seen it, he didn't mention it to her.

"What are you doing here so late?" asked Rhea,

212

surprised.

"I can ask you the same question," he replied with a smile.

Was he listening to her conversation with her father? She had not realized that he had arrived at the clinic. *Had he seen her enter the village and come to check on her but didn't want to say so?* He was never the one to be untowardly emotional, just like her. But the fact that he cared enough to check on her made Rhea feel much better now that she was missing her family after speaking to her father. She locked the clinic and followed him as he walked through the village, which was now thankfully bathed in darkness, which made it impossible for any of the villagers to notice her. He waded them across the river into his parked van on the other side. They drove in silence, a silence that felt strangely comfortable.

"So you knew all along," said Rhea, breaking the silence after a while.

She had figured out that he already knew what had happened at White Arc from his unsurprised reaction after the minister's revelation.

"Yes," replied Saahil, keeping his eyes on the road.

"How?" asked Rhea.

"I googled your name, and it came up in one result," he said sheepishly.

"Why?" asked Rhea.

"Because I was curious," said Saahil. "I was curious why a good-looking, well-educated surgeon had left a well-paying job in her city and come here on a solo trip only to stay back and help out the people."

Saahil didn't believe in making up stories to impress someone. He believed in stating facts, just like her. She remembered how he was suspicious about her when they had just met, which is why he had looked her up. They remained quiet again as Rhea contemplated what he had just said. *Did no one believe that what she had done in Tashkar had nothing to do with her life in Mumbai?*

"I have decided to go back home," revealed Rhea.

Saahil didn't respond. He just kept driving with his eyes firmly on the road.

"Where are you taking me?" asked Rhea after a while when she noticed he was not taking the route to her lodge.

"I want to show you something," he said. "You missed one tourist spot."

She found it strange that he was taking her sightseeing of all the places now. *Was it because she said she was leaving?* They drove for another 15 minutes, coursing through a hilly area, and stopped at a large open platform with the Indian flag hoisted high above it. The open platform had an archway on which was inscribed - *Hall Of Fame*. Rhea followed Saahil as he walked through the archway and then made his way silently around the open platform. In the darkness, she could see several coloured flags hoisted along the sides of the parapet.

"What is this place?" asked Rhea.

"This is a museum constructed by the Indian army in memory of the brave Indian soldiers who died defending our country in the Indo-Pak war," he said.

They strolled along the parapet and settled on one end. The grey clouds above rushed, blocking out the stars beyond them. The flags flapped in the chilly breeze, and Rhea held her sweater tight and pulled her knees to her chest. She could see a section of Leh illuminated by lights from their position. She could also catch a glimpse of Tashkar in the darkness.

"Those news reports were true," said Rhea, even

though Saahil had not asked. "I operated on unnecessary cases. I operated on a dead patient, too. I don't know why I did it. Probably because I was dead inside myself."

Saahil kept looking in the distance at the village of Tashkar, nodding silently.

"But whatever I did here in Tashkar has nothing to do with my past. It started with me following you that night because I was angry with you, and I saw you carrying a knife. I wanted to catch you red-handed doing something wrong because you humiliated me. Instead, I ended up knowing your family's secret. And that made me want to help you, Sania, and Shainaz for the love your family showered me with. I started teaching the kids as a challenge to myself; I took up the *ice stupa* project as a challenge to the minister. It started with me challenging my ego, and it ended with me loving the villagers so much that I enjoyed helping them out," said Rhea.

Saahil listened patiently, allowing Rhea to talk her heart out.

"Never did I think that helping Tashkar would cleanse my sins of the past because until now, I had never accepted that I had done something wrong. Never did I think I would use this village as a platform to showcase myself as a good person to the world; it just happened unintentionally," said Rhea.

Saahil looked at her for the first time. His handsome features, which used to be contorted into a scowl when they had just met, had softened over time. She saw earnestness and respect for her in his eyes. He was not a man of words.

"Come with me," he said and stood up.

He walked to the statue of Lord Buddha, which was laid in front of the Hall of Fame, followed by Rhea. Lord Buddha's idol was seated with a halo behind his head with a serene expression. Below it was an inscription - *It is better to conquer yourself than win a thousand battles. Then the victory is yours. It cannot be taken from you, not by angels nor by demons, heaven or hell.*

It was indeed an apt message for her, and Rhea realized the real reason Saahil had brought her there.

"Not even for a minute did I doubt your intentions behind helping the people of Tashkar, even though I already knew the truth of your past by then," he said. "People have come and gone, but you are the first person who has stood up for the people here. You have fought for them and made a difference in their lives, and nothing about your past can tarnish that fact."

Rhea listened as he spoke to her for the first time in more than a sentence.

"Whatever you have done in your past might have been wrong, and you can't change that, nor can you justify it. But what is more important is, just like the message says here, that you have to conquer the past and come out as a better person. And if you have, you should embrace it and not let anyone make you feel less of a person," he said.

He was right. She had done wrong in a different place, at a different time. But she was no longer that person. She had made a brand new start and had to see that she continued it.

"Thank you!" she said and embraced him warmly.

Chapter Twenty-Three

Rhea arrived in Tashkar the following day with a newfound purpose and energy. She requested that Shainaz, Saahil, and Sania come with her since she had an important announcement. Upon reaching the village square, Rhea asked all the children attending classes there to go back home and inform their parents and the rest of the villagers to gather there. She even requested Sania to tell the headman that she wanted him to assemble with the villagers since she had something important to say. Soon, the village square was filled with a buzz of curiosity as everyone wanted to know why Rhea had summoned them. She waited until the headman made his way to the back of the crowd to begin her announcement.

"Good morning, everybody," Rhea said. "You must all be wondering why this killer doctor has gathered you all today."

The open use of the word *killer* silenced the buzz in the crowd.

"First of all, let me confirm that whatever the minister said about my past is true," said Rhea.

She waited as the surprised villagers began murmuring again.

"But whatever happened after I landed in Leh was not how the minister portrayed it. Let me tell you honestly that when I first saw the harsh living conditions in Tashkar, the first thought that came to my mind was not to help you but to run as far away as possible from you all," said Rhea.

The children looked at her, surprised. Until then, they thought Rhea loved them from the start.

"Why would I want to stay here? I was raised in a comfortable place with all the facilities available to lead a good life. So staying here with you people was out of the question. And I even told Saahil the same during one of our many fights when I landed here," said Rhea.

Saahil stood with his arms crossed over his chest, a smile playing on his lips, while his gaze remained fixed on the ground.

"Then I learned about Saahil and Sania and how their father betrayed you all. How their father betrayed the headman who considered him his best friend, his brother-in-law. I can't imagine the pain that he would have instilled in all your lives," said Rhea.

The headman turned away as if the very thought was painful for him.

"And yet some of you supported his son," said Rhea, looking at Saahil. "And despite some of you hating him, Saahil cared for your children and all the residents of Tashkar. And that was something I could not understand. How can someone do a good deed for someone who has mistreated them?"

"That was what drew me to this village. That is what is special about you all. The people here struggle to survive, yet they help each other. The headman cares for the villagers despite the odds being stacked against him. A terrorist's son is teaching the children here, even though he could not complete his education because of the adversities that he has had to face. A mother is supporting her children all by herself after losing her husband and being asked to leave her village by her brother," said Rhea.

She saw Shainaz smile, clutching Sania's wrist.

"It made me realize that life is not only about competing with others. It is also about living one's life and helping others. The newspapers have shown what I have done for this village but have not shown what you all have done for me in return and how much I have learned from you all. The truth is that Tashkar has changed my life, and I want to thank you all from the depths of my heart for it," said Rhea, teary-eyed.

She went over to Sania and Saahil and hugged them both. As the people watched in awe, the headman walked from the back of the crowd and climbed the platform. He looked at all three of them with an expressionless face.

"As you said, I have been here a long time and witnessed a lot of disappointment over the years, so much so that I had lost the will to be hopeful about anything for my people. That is why I stubbed you when you came to this village. I felt that you were one of those starry-eyed youngsters who thought that changing the world was as easy as changing one's clothes," he said.

Rhea nodded understandingly.

"But as the days passed, I saw that you were different. You never gave up, proving that one can achieve what they set out to do if they put their mind to it. And I admire you for that," he said, folding his hands in respect.

The headman then turned his attention to Saahil and Sania.

"I indeed hated you both from the depths of my heart,"

he said as Sania stared at her feet, and Saahil looked back at him stone-faced.

"I hated you because of your father, for what he did to this village, and, more importantly, for what he did to me. I could not accept the fact that you both were running around this village while my own two children, who would have been your age, were not here because of your father. It seemed unfair," he said.

Rhea could feel the pain behind each word the headman was saying.

"But as Dr Rhea said, no one should be punished for their past sins while doing something good in the present. And here, you both were not even responsible for any sins. And I drove my sister out of this village when she lost her husband and needed me the most. How could I be so heartless? How could I be so selfish? So I fold my hands and ask you for forgiveness in front of my people for how I have treated you and your family," said the old man, joining his hands in apology.

Saahil immediately grabbed the headman's hand, preventing him from apologizing. Sania held his hands, too, as they all wept. The headman then looked at Shainaz, walked to her, and hugged her as both shed tears of joy and relief. A long, painful part of their lives was now well and truly behind them.

#

That night Rhea heard song and dance in Tashkar for the first time since she had arrived a year ago. A huge pyre was lit in the centre of the village square, and the villagers indulged in traditional songs and dances. Both the children and the adults took part, and soon, Rhea was pulled amongst them. At first, she found it hard since she had not danced in a long time, but with Sania's help, she slowly got the hang of it, and once she did, she let her hair loose and thoroughly enjoyed herself.

After an hour of dancing, they all sat on the bare ground breathless, relishing the kebab being cooked in the pyre right before them.

"I have never had so much fun, *didi*," said Sania, wiping the sweat off her brow even during the evening chill.

"Nor have I," said Rhea, sipping water off her thermos.

"What a difference you have made to the lives of these people. And to our lives, *didi*," Sania said.

Their eyes went spontaneously to the *ice stupa*, which had grown almost to a height of 30 feet and whose peak was visible from where they were seated.

"The ice stupa was a great initiative," admitted Rhea. "But the media coverage that followed it, voter registration, construction of the bridge, and electricity would not have been possible if Divya had not put that video of yours online."

"Yes *didi*," said Sania. "Those videos turned out to be magic for this village."

That night, when Rhea was in bed in her hotel room, which was now like a second home to her, Sania's words echoed in her ears. *Those videos were like magic to this village.*

Indeed, those videos had changed the village's landscape, and Rhea was more thankful than ever that Divya had uploaded them. But now she thought there was one more thing she could do before she left Tashkar and Leh. She would need to call the expert to know how to do it and clear all her doubts.

"Hello, stranger," said her brother, Rahul. "How come the celebrity remembered me all of a sudden?"

"It's not like you have been calling me daily to check

on me," mocked Rhea. "How is work going?"

"It's going great," said her brother. "By the way, are you planning ever to return home?"

Both of them laughed. They chatted for a while, catching up on each other's life. The last time she spoke to him was when her name was mentioned in the newspapers for the ice stupa, and he called to congratulate her.

"Listen, I called you up because I wanted to know something," said Rhea.

"And here I assumed you called up to check on your little brother," he joked.

"I wanted to know how I could upload a few videos on social media," said Rhea, ignoring his jibe.

"Do you want to go viral again? How hungry for fame are you?" he laughed.

"Stop clowning around," she scolded him. "These videos are not mine."

"Oh! Upload them on your Facebook account if you want people to see them," he said.

"What Facebook account?" asked Rhea.

"The one your brother created for you back when you wanted to promote your practice before you became a celebrity," he said.

Rhea had long forgotten about that account. It was as if it was in another life.

"I had forgotten about that," said Rhea.

He then guided her on how to upload the videos. She had even forgotten the password, but thankfully he remembered. She then uploaded the videos that she wanted and went to bed.

#

"What did you do?" asked a visibly excited Saahil.

222

"I did nothing. I have been sitting here chatting with Sania since morning," a surprised Rhea replied.

"My office has been inundated with calls for bookings with special requests for stops at *Shainaz's Kitchen* and pictures with tour guide Sania," he said, bewildered.

Sania looked at her wide-eyed, and Rhea could not contain her laughter looking at her shell-shocked face. It had been three days since she uploaded Sania's videos on her Facebook account, the same videos she had captured while Sania was explaining various tourist spots in Leh Ladakh. After she had uploaded them, she checked her Facebook account multiple times a day and saw that the videos were generating a lot of curiosity. She opened her account on her phone and showed them both the comments and likes the videos were garnering.

"So many people saw my videos?" asked Sania incredulously.

"You are a star, Sania! They love your videos. You have a flair for talking in front of people," said Rhea.

"I am scared to talk in front of ten people except for the children here," said Sania.

"And yet thousands are watching your videos and appreciating you," said Rhea.

The next few weeks were hectic for Saahil, Shainaz, and Sania. Though Rhea was supposed to leave, they requested that she stay a few more days to see the outcome of her videos. Saahil's agency was overwhelmed with customers who wanted Sania as their tour guide. *Shainaz's Kitchen* became a tourist destination, with people wanting to try out the delicacies and clicking pictures in front of the eatery with Shainaz. Rhea was relishing their success. It was all and more they deserved for everything they had been through.

Chapter Twenty-Four

Rhea, Saahil, and Sania were crouched behind a boulder high in the mountains in the chill of the night. Luckily for Rhea, Saahil had warned her about the expedition in advance, so she was dressed in multiple layers of clothing to keep her warm.

"How is it that no matter how much I try, I can never feel warm enough in Leh?" asked Rhea.

"Maybe because we are just thick-skinned people," whispered Sania, giggling.

"Shhh…" said Saahil as he craned his neck and squinted in the darkness at the pipes leading to the *ice stupa*.

The three of them arrived at the location an hour ago and concealed themselves in the darkness. Accompanying them were about ten villagers who had climbed up the mountains secretly as a backup. Saahil had received intel that a group of men would arrive in the dead of the night to destroy the pipes, just like they had done a few months ago. He had told Rhea that he would hide in the dark to capture them along with a few villagers. Both Rhea and Sania had insisted on joining him.

"I don't think they will come," said Sania. "They probably spotted us as we made our way up the mountain and fled."

"They will definitely spot us if you keep opening your

mouth," scolded Saahil.

Sania stuck her tongue out at him, which made Rhea smile and realize how young and childish Sania was. Suddenly, the silence was broken by a snapping twig under someone's foot. Rhea became tense, and the muscles in Saahil's forearms tightened. She was grateful that he hadn't brought his rifle and had only carried an iron rod. They waited for a while and saw the silhouettes of four men. One turned off the valve that supplied water to the trench below, while two others took tools from their rucksack and began cutting the pipes. The fourth man was serving as a lookout, unaware of their presence.

Saahil waited for a while, and when he had gathered sufficient evidence of sabotage, he let out a loud battle cry. All the villagers joined him in attacking the intruders. The intruders were unaware and unarmed, with only tools available for their defence, so they were helpless against the collective strength and fury of the villagers. Soon enough, they were apprehended and taken to the village for further action.

"Who sent you here?" growled Saahil once they were at the village square.

By then, the entire village had been alerted, and the villagers had all made their way to the village square with fire lanterns in hand. The man being questioned looked at the ground, unwilling to answer.

"Who sent you here?" shouted Saahil again.

Again, the four perpetrators remained silent and defiant.

"Last chance," said Saahil, "Or I set all of you on fire one by one."

Rhea had no doubts he was angry enough to make good his claims, and the same thought perhaps crossed the miscreants' minds as well.

"Ministerji…Ministerji," shouted the man Saahil had directed the fire lantern towards.

The entire village gasped, but the revelation didn't surprise Rhea, Saahil & Sania.

#

A visibly angry Bhadrapala made his way to the village square the following day when he was informed that someone had accused him of sabotaging the *ice stupa* in Tashkar. He was accompanied by Tenzin and his men, who marched into the village with vengeance. The villagers had tied up the four miscreants to trees despite Rhea's objections. They had already gathered around when they had heard that the minister would be coming. When the minister saw the men tied to the trees, he was incensed.

"Who tied these men?" he growled.

"I did," said Saahil, stepping forward.

"And who gave you the permission to disperse the law of the land?" demanded the minister, pointing a finger at him.

"Who permitted you to sabotage this village?" demanded Rhea.

If Bhadrapala was not already livid, he was now furious. His aides moved forward intimidatingly towards Rhea and Saahil but had to back down when they saw all the villagers move behind them in support. Tenzin sobbed silently beside her father. His ploy of bringing his daughter along to appease the villagers had clearly run its course and no longer affected them, though she had no part to play in his misdemeanours.

"And what proof do you have that I had anything to do with this?" the minister asked.

"The men admitted that you sent them," Rhea retorted.

"Oh, that's all, is it?" asked the minister, laughing aloud. "Four men say that I have done it, and you all believe it? I can bring 100 people here who say I haven't done anything."

Rhea could not believe his nerve that he could lie so openly and defend himself.

"I think you hired these men to defame me and fool the villagers," said Bhadrapala.

"Yes!" shouted one man tied to the tree. "She hired us to sabotage the pipes, get caught, and blame ministerji."

Both Saahil and Rhea looked at each other, stupefied. They knew the men were lying to protect the minister. They seemed to have found their tongue when he was amidst them. How could he stoop so low? Wasn't there an ounce of morality in him? *Is he as bad as I was back at White Arc,* wondered Rhea.

Before Rhea could reply, they heard gunshots in the distance. Rhea heard something whiz past her.

"Shelling!" yelled the villagers, and they started running toward the safety of their homes.

"Shelling is over at the hills. What are you cowards running for?" Bhadrapala shouted angrily.

Rhea heard a soft cry. Both Bhadrapala and she turned to look at the same time. Tenzin was standing with a look of surprise and pain on her face, clutching her abdomen. Rhea's eyes travelled from her face to her abdomen, and she saw her white salwar kameez slowly turning red. That's when Rhea realized what the whizzing sound was. Tenzin had been shot.

#

Bhadrapala reached Tenzin first and began screaming incoherently for help. His aides stood in disbelief, unable to

227

comprehend what they should do next. Rhea hurried towards Tenzin and knelt beside her as she gasped for breath, the spot of blood on her salwar kameez growing by the second.

"Somebody give me a cloth to stop the bleeding," screamed Rhea.

Sania took off her hijab, handed it over, and scampered to the clinic to fetch the first aid kit. Rhea pressed the hijab hard over Tenzin's abdomen to stop the bleeding.

"We need to get her to the hospital right away," commanded Rhea.

"Can't we do something here at your clinic?" the minister pleaded. "Traveling to the hospital would take time."

"We don't have the facility to operate here, and she needs surgery right away," Rhea replied angrily, not understanding how stupid he could be to ask such a question.

"How can we make it? The walk through the trees, the river..." his voice trailed off.

Before Bhadrapala could complete his sentence, Saahil knelt beside them, lifted Tenzin in his arms, and began running towards the river. Rhea and Sania followed, having brought the mops from the clinic and replaced the hijab on Tenzin's abdomen with them.

"Stay with me, Tenzin. You are a brave girl," said Rhea, and Tenzin responded with a nod, though her eyes appeared glazed.

They rushed through the mangrove trees, and Saahil, Tenzin, Rhea, and Sania got into the boat. The minister joined them, panting as well. Saahil placed Tenzin in Rhea's lap and waded them across the river as fast as possible. By the time they reached Saahil's minivan, Tenzin was pale.

They got into the minivan, and Saahil helped Rhea place Tenzin in the backseat with her head on her father's lap.

Rhea sat on the floor beside her, pressing the mops on her abdomen, which were now glistening bright red.

Saahil started the vehicle and drove it towards the hospital at breakneck speed. Rhea asked Sania to place her hand on the mops on Tenzin's abdomen while she inserted the IV cannula that Sania had brought from the clinic into Tenzin's wrist. She then connected it to a fluid bottle and pressed it to rush the fluid into her veins. It would help to temporarily maintain her blood pressure. By the time they reached the hospital, Rhea had emptied one bottle and inserted the second one.

Once at the hospital, Tenzin was wheeled into the same emergency section that Rhea was brought to a year ago when she had fallen and hurt herself at the Zanskar trek. It was ironic that both times, Saahil had carried the victim in his arms to the hospital.

"Arrange two bottles of blood, prepare the operation theatre, and inform the surgeon. She needs to undergo emergency surgery," Rhea ordered the doctor, who greeted them.

The patient's sudden arrival created pandemonium in the hospital. The duty doctor and the nurse ran helter-skelter, unable to comprehend Rhea's instructions. Bhadrapala screamed at everyone, looking at the sad state of affairs at the government-run hospital.

"The surgeon will take an hour to reach here," said the duty doctor warily to the Bhadrapala.

"What do you mean he will take an hour to reach? He is supposed to be here all the time," he screamed.

The duty doctor looked down at the floor, too scared to answer. Rhea knew the modus operandi. The surgeon was probably operating in a private hospital far away during his duty hours in the government hospital to compensate for the poor wages there.

"Get someone else then," commanded Rhea.

"There is no one else," said the duty doctor.

Bhadrapala grabbed the duty doctor by his collar with both hands and drew him close to his face.

"You better get me a surgeon immediately," he said menacingly.

"I am sorry, sir. We have no one else," said the duty doctor forlorn.

He let go of him and looked at his daughter lying on the stretcher with Rhea's hand on her abdomen. She was as pale as paper. The sight drained the life out of him, and he suddenly broke down and fell beside her helplessly. Rhea was caught off guard briefly by the sudden change in his demeanour. *How had such a powerful man turned so vulnerable?*

"*Didi*, you can operate on her, right?" asked Sania, kneeling beside Rhea.

Rhea noticed Bhadrapala's sudden expression of surprise as he looked up on hearing Sania.

"I had completely forgotten that you were a surgeon," he said, looking at Rhea.

"I am not allowed to operate since my license has been cancelled," said Rhea

"Screw the law!" screamed Bhadrapala. "My daughter's life is at stake here."

For a moment, Rhea was caught unaware by the sudden turn of events. The thought of operating on Tenzin had never crossed her mind. It had been a year since she had last wielded a scalpel; legally speaking, she wasn't allowed to operate. *Was the cancellation of her license reason enough for her to let a little girl lose her life?* Hadn't Rhea broken the rules for questionable purposes earlier? Then why was she thinking twice about breaking a rule to save a life? Indeed, she could not worry about rules in such a situation. The minister's desperation and Rhea's fondness for Tenzin made up her mind for her.

The task suddenly rejuvenated her, and she took charge of the situation. She ordered Tenzin to be shifted to the operation theatre immediately. All the arrangements were made within a few minutes, and Tenzin was put under general anaesthesia.

Just before Rhea was about to enter the operation theatre, Bhadrapala approached her. He looked haggard with red, puffy eyes. Gone was the authoritarian minister who made false promises and bullied people around him.

"Please save my daughter," he said, joining his hands and breaking down completely, holding Rhea's hands.

For Rhea, it was a moment of deja vu, bringing back memories of the mother and wife who had begged her to save her to save their patient. In the minister, she saw the mother who had joined her hands and put her trust in her. Not only had Rhea failed, but she had also cheated them.

"I will do my best," said Rhea, patting him on his shoulder and turning to the OT.

Standing next to Tenzin to begin the surgery, she remembered their good times together. She was a bright, curious girl who fervently desired to become a doctor someday. She taught the village children regularly until her father had ended it. Her life and future were now in Rhea's hands. Rhea had a policy of never being personally involved with her patients, but it was too late for that here. And to top it off, it had been almost a year since she had operated on a patient.

But she was Dr Rhea Sharma, one of the best surgeons. If there was anyone who could save Tenzin, it was her. She put aside all her thoughts. It was time.

"Scalpel, please," she said.

Chapter Twenty-Five

Sania was devastated and hadn't stopped crying since the previous night. Rhea tried her best to console her but could not hold back her tears. Shainaz was beside them, caressing Rhea's cheek overwhelmed with emotion. Saahil stood in a corner away from everyone, hands in pockets, too proud and masculine to admit that he was distraught. The villagers had all gathered around them, and grown men and women with their children were crying inconsolably. The headman stood silently with arms crossed, watching Sania and Rhea.

It had been three weeks since Tenzin's surgery and just over a year now since Rhea had first set foot in Leh as a tourist embarking on a two-week holiday to get away from the nightmare her life had turned into after losing her job and license to practice and being branded a *killer* doctor in the local media. The Rhea who had arrived in Leh drastically differed from the one standing and holding a bawling Sania now. She had learned so much in the past year that she felt like she was a different person altogether. Though she was still aggressive, competent, and bold, her perspective on life had changed dramatically.

Rhea was finally ready to head back home. When she

arrived in Leh, she had no idea what the future held for her after a year. However, now she had a clear idea of what she wanted to do once she returned home. The first item on her agenda was to sit down with her parents and brother to discuss her plans. Rhea was eager to see her family again, as she missed them dearly. She was grateful to have two families, one in Mumbai and the other in Tashkar.

"Promise me you will pick up my calls and not be too busy or forget me, *didi*," cried Sania.

"Shut up, you stupid girl," said Rhea tearfully. "Not only will I pick up your calls, but I will also call you up myself and keep coming back here to visit you all."

"Next time you come, please bring your family as well," said Shainaz, embracing her warmly.

"I will, and I want all three of you to visit me in Mumbai," said Rhea.

"The village of Tashkar will always welcome you with open arms," said a voice behind them.

Rhea spun around and saw the headman standing in a maroon goncha. His wrinkled and desolate face conveyed a deep sense of sadness. She couldn't help but feel touched by his fondness for her.

"I know," she said, "Tashkar is my second home."

Just then, a beaming Bhadrapala arrived with Tenzin by his side. The smile had not left his face ever since Tenzin's surgery. For a change, he was not accompanied by his aides. Tenzin walked gingerly, holding her abdomen. Her surgery had been a success, and after Rhea had removed the bullet that had lodged in her spleen, Bhadrapala considered Rhea God-sent. Her recovery had gone well, and she had been discharged a week ago.

"*Didi*!" she said and hugged her.

"How is my most favourite patient in the whole wide world?" asked Rhea, hugging her.

"I am perfectly fine," replied Tenzin.

"And it is all thanks to you," said Bhadrapala. "I shudder to think what would have happened if you weren't with us that day."

"I just did my job," said Rhea.

But deep inside, she knew it was more than just a job since Tenzin was more than patient with her.

"And you made me realize that I haven't been doing mine," said Bhadrapala.

With that, he then faced the villagers with folded hands.

"I have made many mistakes in my life, and one among them is to use the people of Tashkar for my benefit. When my daughter was shot and then saved by a person whom I had been targeting unjustly for the past few months, it made me realize how small a person I am. This woman has come to this village and done more for you all in a short period than I have been able to do in the last ten years, and I hang my head in shame. And for this reason, I have decided to withdraw my candidature from the upcoming elections so that someone more capable can win and do justice to you," he declared.

The villagers looked at each other surprised, and whispers rippled through the crowd.

"I don't agree with that at all," said Rhea, surprising the minister.

"I have made too many mistakes to be corrected," replied Bhadrapala.

"You may have committed mistakes in the past, but life gives us all a second chance," said Rhea. "Whatever you have done before will remind you never to be that person again. Try and make a difference now. Nobody knows this village better than you, so you will be the best person to help them rather than someone new."

"I agree with Dr Rhea," said the headman, looking at Bhadrapala. "We will support you wholeheartedly; this time, you don't have to distribute freebies to the villagers."

"Except for sweets after you win," said Rhea.

Bhadrapala nodded in approval and folded his hands again in humility.

Rhea walked and stood in front of Saahil.

"Are you not going to say anything nasty to me before I leave?" she asked, smiling. "For old times' sake."

"You are just a tourist," Saahil said with a wink. "If not, you would've stayed."

"Ouch!" said Rhea, giggling. "That stung"

They hugged. Rhea then turned around, said one last goodbye, and walked slowly out of Tashkar.

#

The airplane took off and continued to ascend. Rhea gazed out the window and watched as the snow-capped mountains receded with each passing second until they appeared like icicles. She recalled looking down at those very icicles when she arrived in Leh over a year ago. She had never imagined that those mountains would have such a profound impact on her life. Now, her life was forever etched in those mountains, leaving an indelible mark. She peered below, hoping to spot Tashkar, but the plane was flying too high for her to see. Nonetheless, it didn't matter because the village was deeply embedded in her heart.

#

Rhea had been expecting a warm welcome from her parents and brother at the airport, and she was not disappointed. As soon as she arrived at the visitor's lounge, she spotted them waving eagerly at her. Her father was holding a *Welcome Home* sign, and her mother was tapping his arm, looking slightly embarrassed by his antics. Rahul was using his smartphone to record a video of her arrival.

What she didn't expect was to be greeted by a posse of her school & college friends, cousins, and other relatives. They had all arrived to give her a grand welcome and made so much noise that everyone looked in her direction, wondering if she was a celebrity. Rhea was mortified and tried to disappear amongst the crowd of passengers. But she soon realized that it was useless, and instead, the embarrassment gave way to joy, and she too couldn't help but be happy to see them all.

The festivities moved to their apartment, and the entire day turned out to be one big celebration with everyone crashing into her apartment. Her mother laid out a feast, basking in everyone's appreciation. It was late at night when everyone left, and a thoroughly exhausted Rhea sprawled on the living room couch after freshening up. Her father joined her.

"It's so nice to be back, Dad," she said, looking at him.

It felt nice to talk to him face-to-face rather than on the phone.

"Strange coming from someone who didn't want to return home for a year," chuckled her father.

Rhea laughed, too. She knew he was only pulling her leg.

"But I really missed you all, Dad," she said.

"We know that," he replied, "And we missed you too."

She sat on the armrest of his rocking chair, just like

she used to when she was a kid.

"So, have you decided what you want to do next?" asked her father.

"As a matter of fact, I have," she said. "And I want to know your opinion about it."

She told him what she had planned for her future.

"That trip has really opened your eyes," said her father, clutching her wrists. "I am so proud of you."

#

Rhea entered the vast reception area of White Arc Hospital, which was bustling with activity as usual. It had been over a year since she had last visited the premises. The high ceilings, the marble floor, the familiar smell of iodoform, the registration area with multiple counters, and doctors in white aprons rushing around the crowd, nothing seemed to have changed. Even the help desk personnel, who used to redirect her patients to Dr Nathwani, was still there. He looked sheepishly at her when she smiled at him. The hospital's personalized service was evident, with the hospital escorts accompanying the patients to the respective departments. She compared it to the run-down condition of Leh Medical Centre, where even a surgeon was not available during an emergency. The people here didn't know how fortunate they were to have access to such top-notch medical facilities.

She wore an all-black skirt suit, which she hadn't worn in over a year. She had become so accustomed to traditional lehengas or multiple layers of clothing that wearing a suit felt out of place. As she walked through the corridor, her heels clicked against the cold, hard floor, triggering memories of everything she had done there for three years. The surgeries she had performed, the patients she had treated, the nursing staff she had scolded, and the numerous times she had thrown surgical instruments in the operation theatre. She winced as if it physically hurt to remember how insensitive she had been to others' feelings back then, as she was consumed with the intense desire to be the best.

She saw a couple of surprised faces stare back at her, but no one came to talk to her. *Were they scared to speak to a killer?* But it didn't bother her. She walked straight to the elevator and got into it. As always, when the elevator stopped on the 6th floor, it seemed like a whole other world from the one down below. The dim overhead orange lights replaced the bright white LEDs. A thick, intricately woven maroon carpet muffled the sounds of her heels against the marble floor. She walked to the receptionist outside Dr Gupta's cabin, who smiled politely.

"They are waiting for you, doctor," she said professionally.

Rhea smiled and entered. Dr Subhash Gupta, the MD of White Arc, and Dr Ishwar Nathwani, the surgical gastroenterologist, were waiting for her in the massive office of the MD. The previous day, she had called Dr. Gupta seeking an appointment and had dialled Dr. Nathwani after that, requesting him to be present, too.

"Good evening, Dr Rhea," said the MD with a plastered smile. "It's so nice to see you after so long."

"Same here, sir," said Rhea.

Dr Nathwani offered the seat next to him, and she settled down on the comfortable upholstered leather chair.

"You have been making a name for yourself up north, right?" said Dr Nathwani.

It was hard to know if he was complimenting her or being sarcastic.

"I don't know about that," said Rhea, chuckling.

She was pleased to see that they were at least keeping track of her activities even after she had been let go.

"Yes, you were the talk of the town after you brought some changes in a God-forsaken village," said Dr Gupta, adjusting his gold-rimmed spectacles and leaning backward on his chair.

"Tashkar," said Rhea.

"Sorry?" he asked, confused.

"The God-forsaken village's name is Tashkar," she said with a smile.

Both noticed that though she was smiling, her voice was stern.

"Anyway, let's get to the point," said Dr. Gupta, leaning forward on his table, as usual, not wasting time with small talk. "You called me yesterday to set up this appointment. Though you didn't tell me what this meeting was for, I assume you want to work with us again."

Rhea smiled, which Dr. Gupta interpreted as a signal to continue.

"Now that you have reclaimed your license to practice after serving your one-year penalty, it would delight us to have you back on our team," said Dr. Gupta.

His offer surprised Rhea, considering how badly he wanted to get rid of her once her name was flashed in the media a year ago. She wondered why he seemed so eager to have her back.

"With your recent accomplishments, you have gained some popularity, which could attract more patients to the hospital," he said without missing a beat.

Rhea smiled again. *So that was the reason.* Dr Gupta being the business executive as always.

"But I haven't come here to join back," said Rhea. "I

came for something else."

Both Dr Gupta and Dr Nathwani were taken aback by her response, and she enjoyed the look on their faces.

"My intention of coming here was to invite you both to the opening of my new clinic," Rhea said, pulling two invites from her bag and handing them over to them.

They both took their respective invites and scrutinized them.

"But why do you want to open a clinic when you have a ready-made set-up right here?" asked Dr Gupta. "You do not know how difficult it is to work as a solo practitioner without a set-up in a metro like Mumbai."

"I know it's very tough," said Rhea, smiling. "But I want to work for myself and my patients without being put under pressure by anyone else,"

"You will earn much more with us," interjected Dr Nathwani.

Rhea laughed.

"I haven't earned a rupee in the last year yet am happy. In fact, right now, I am happier than when I was earning bucket loads working here. Back then, I had money but no time for myself or my family. The last year has taught me to love myself and enjoy my life and work. So I intend to balance my work and free time, and I can do that only if I am my boss," Rhea said, smiling.

Dr Nathwani looked lost for words. Dr Gupta knew that the last statement was directed towards him, and he, too, chose not to respond.

"And I want you both to inaugurate the clinic," said Rhea.

Both Dr Gupta and Dr Nathwani looked stunned. *Why on earth would she want them to inaugurate her clinic?* After all, it was under their pressure that Rhea buckled and made decisions that ruined her life. And they were then responsible for her ouster from White Arc. Instead of coming to her aid, they had looked the other way. And now she wanted them to inaugurate her new venture, which would start a new chapter in her life. Rhea read their thoughts.

"I want you to inaugurate it because if it wasn't for you, I wouldn't have left this life of mine and travelled. And if I hadn't travelled, I wouldn't have discovered the village of Tashkar. And it was that discovery that has now changed my life completely. So, in a way, you both made me realize what I truly wanted in life," she said.

Neither Dr. Gupta nor Dr. Nathwani had anything to say to her. Rhea stood up and thanked them. Then she left the chamber, feeling more liberated and happy than ever.

#

Sania was standing, staring at the wall in front of her, clutching her pink hijab. She couldn't believe what she was seeing. Dressed in a pink pantsuit, Rhea stood beside her, grinning from ear to ear as she looked at Sania's shocked expression. The wall was covered in tiny portraits depicting places in Leh and Tashkar. Each picture represented a memory Rhea had of that place, and since Sania was a big part of those memories, she was present in most of the pictures, standing beside Rhea. The portraits included images of the Zanskar River, Shanti Stupa, Shey Palace, Hall of Fame, Magnetic Hill, Shainaz Kitchen, and Ice Stupa. In addition, there were pictures of the children of Tashkar, the headman, Saahil, Bhadrapala, and Tenzin.

The most prominent among them were several pictures of Tashkar and the clinic. After all, the wall was a part of Rhea's tiny clinic in Mumbai. She had organized a small inauguration ceremony for which she had insisted that Shainaz, Saahil, and Sania be present, and they had arrived for the same, which delighted Rhea to no end. Divya was there, too. But undoubtedly the loudest and the most prominent among the guests was *Sardarji,* who stood out not only because of his bright attire but also because he had brought an eight-member band playing live music and bhangra outside the clinic.

"Oye madamji, Tashkar in Mumbai! What kind of *jugaad* is this?" he said, clearly thrilled.

"*Sardarji* is right. You have two Tashkar clinics," said Divya, holding Rhea's arm. "Talk about being an entrepreneur."

"That too in two different states," said Rhea, laughing.

"So, how exactly have you planned this?" asked Divya. "It must be a big change from working at White Arc, where the pay was higher, the facilities were innumerable, and you had everything at your beck and call,"

"Yes, it's a big change, but the right one," said Rhea. I plan to see patients here in my clinic and then operate on the ones who need surgery in a nearby hospital, where they are charged reasonably. At first, the work might not be as much as it used to be at White Arc, but at least I'll have time for myself. And every few months, I plan to visit Leh and Tashkar and check how the clinic is running."

"That is the best part of the plan, *didi,*" said Sania, pouncing in.

All three of them laughed.

"You better take good care of the clinic there when I am away," said Rhea, pinching Sania's arm.

"I will, *didi.* With Tenzin's help, we'll see that we care for whoever visits the clinic".

"Saahil and I will help, too," said Shainaz, joining them.

Rhea's parents joined the group, and her father was beaming from ear to ear.

"You must be so proud of your daughter. She came and changed our lives," said Shainaz, holding Rhea's hand.

"I have always been proud of her," said her father.

Rhea went and hugged him. He was always her biggest supporter.

"Are there any good marriage proposals there for her?" Rhea's mother asked, as always out of context.

Divya burst into laughter, assuming Rhea's mother was joking, but when she saw the serious expression on her face, she felt embarrassed. Rhea chuckled at her reaction.

"Let's have a picture to go on the wall," said the photographer, breaking the awkwardness. Everyone huddled together.

Rhea's parents, her brother, Shainaz, Sania, Saahil, Divya, and Sardarji all stood together and huddled around Rhea.

It was the best picture of the lot, and it would become the centrepiece on the wall of photographs.

* * *

ACKNOWLEDGEMENTS

First of all, if you are holding this book, it means you have picked something that I have put a lot of thought and effort into and I thank you for it.

I thank my friends Avakash Chand, Pradyumna Bhandary, and Edward Prashanth, with whom my journey as an author began when I wrote my first book, OUR IMPERFECT STORY, a book they helped create.

My heartfelt gratitude to Dr Sharanya Shetty for managing surgery Unit 5 when I would get lost in this book.

The cover of this book has been designed by Dr Kashyap Anand, who has done an exceptional job and I really appreciate it.

My parents, Hermy Fernandes & Louis Fernandes, and my sister, Megan D'Souza, for always being there for me.

Amazon.com for providing a platform for amateur authors like me to get our stories read by thousands of readers.

Notion Press and their Xpress Publishing resources through which this paperback was published.

Finally, I would like to express my gratitude towards my wife, Dr. Nishita Fernandes, for her unwavering support. I am also grateful to my sons, Nihaan and Evaan, for inspiring me to write books like this one. My hope is that someday they will read it and understand the message that I want to convey to them.

ABOUT THE AUTHOR

Ryan Fernandes hails from the beautiful coastal city of Mangalore, Karnataka. He is currently working as a Professor in the Department of Surgery at a reputed medical college.

He is a surgeon by profession, an author, a self-proclaimed cricket expert and a Formula one aficionado. He is an online educator having taught MBBS & post graduate students on various platforms.

He is a voracious reader with a keen interest in writing. His first novel, *Our Imperfect Story* inspired by various real-life incidents was published in 2020

This is his second novel.

You can follow him on:
Instagram : ryanfernandes.in
Facebook : ryanfernandes.face
Twitter : _ryanfernandes_
Email: ryan_fernandes@zohomail.com

www.ingramcontent.com/pod-product-compliance
Lightning Source LLC
Chambersburg PA
CBHW060528160726
47991CB00001B/231